W9-ARX-330

I'll Sing You Two-O

ANTHEA FRASER

I'll Sing You Two-O

St. Martin's Press ☙ New York

MYS
F841 2iL

A THOMAS DUNNE BOOK.
An imprint of St. Martin's Press.

I'LL SING YOU TWO-O. Copyright © 1991 by Anthea Fraser.

Library of Congress Cataloging-in-Publication Data

Fraser, Anthea.
    I'll sing you two-O / by Anthea Fraser.
        p.   cm.
    "A Thomas Dunne book."
    ISBN 0-312-14623-X
    I. Title.
    PR6056.R286I4   1996
    823'.914—dc20   96-27971
                                               CIP

First published in Great Britain by the Crime Club,
an imprint of HarperCollins Publishers

First U.S. Edition: December 1996

10   9   8   7   6   5   4   3   2   1

To Ian, who's been waiting for this one,
with love as always.

I'll Sing You Two-O

GREEN GROW THE RUSHES-O

I'll sing you one-O!
(*Chorus*) Green grow the rushes-O!
        What is your one-O?
One is one and all alone and evermore shall be so.

I'll sing you two-O!
(*Chorus*) Green grow the rushes-O!
        What are your two-O?
Two, two, the lily-white Boys, clothed all in green-O,
(*Chorus*) One is one and all alone and evermore shall be so.

I'll sing you three-O!
(*Chorus*) Green grow the rushes-O!
        What are your three-O?
Three, three the Rivals,
(*Chorus*) Two, two, the lily-white Boys,
clothed all in green-O,
One is one and all alone and evermore shall be so.

Four for the Gospel-makers.
Five for the Symbols at your door.
Six for the six proud Walkers.
Seven for the seven Stars in the sky.
Eight for the April Rainers.
Nine for the nine bright Shiners.
Ten for the ten Commandments.
Eleven for the Eleven that went up to Heaven.
Twelve for the twelve Apostles.

PROLOGUE

It was a clear night with the moon almost full. They hadn't spoken for some time and, though a reggae band throbbed insistently on the cassette, neither was aware of it until it ended. Then, roused by the sudden silence, Rob said gloatingly, 'Stroke of luck, that.'

'Magic!' Gary agreed. They'd come across it by chance, a large, isolated house, whose open garage door shouted aloud that no one was home. And the alarm hadn't delayed them for a moment. Pathetic! Result, they'd nabbed some good stuff, which Jack would be able to shift for them. All in all, a fitting way to end a day in which United beat Steeple Bayliss four-nil. Last match of the season, too. He gave a sigh of pure contentment.

The country road stretched emptily before and behind them, a glowing ribbon in the moonlight across which occasional shadows of trees lay like giant pencils. Then, as a sound impinged on his musings, he frowned, glancing in the wing mirror. 'Not being followed, are we?' he asked sharply.

Rob wound down his window and, sticking his head out, looked back the way they'd come. 'Nothing in sight.'

But even as he withdrew his head he caught the sound which had alerted his twin, a low, throbbing hum growing steadily louder.

'Plane,' Gary said in relief. 'Pretty low, by the sound of it.'

'Not half!' Rob pointed suddenly to their right, where a dark shape was silhouetted against the sky, seemingly only feet above the treetops. 'He's coming down—and without landing lights, at that. No airfield round here, is there?'

'Not that I've heard of.' Gary pulled the van off the road into the shelter of the trees. 'Let's have a shufty.'

The night air was chill after the warm van, and reverberating with the sound of the plane. Bent almost double, they set off at a loping run through the trees, dodging the straggling branches which snatched at their clothes. The note of the engine had changed and ahead of them a powerful torch flashed once, then twice in quick succession.

Instinctively dropping to their stomachs, the twins inched silently forward until the trees thinned and the flat grassland beyond became visible. And with perfect timing, the plane taxied slowly into sight and came to a standstill.

As its engine died a car, which had been parked out of sight to their left, backed rapidly towards it, braked, and disgorged two figures. One opened the hatchback while the other ran towards the plane, reaching it as the pilot slid back his own door.

For several minutes the three men worked quickly and efficiently, the pilot handing down several dozen packages which were swiftly transferred to the open maw of the car. Hardly any words were spoken, and none reached the watchers under the trees.

In a surprisingly short time the transfer was complete. Doors were closed, the pilot slewed the plane round and set off again along the makeshift runway. As the roar of its going filled the night, the two men walked round to the front of the car. Gary was about to ease himself up for a better look when, with a muttered word to his companion, one of them veered suddenly towards the trees where they lay hidden.

Convinced they'd been spotted, the twins pressed themselves into the ground, pulling their anoraks over their heads and waiting with pounding hearts for retribution to fall. But after an agonizing pause the only sound that reached them was a soft pattering on the shrubs to their left. Limp with relief, they exchanged grins. The man had merely taken the chance to relieve himself.

As he finished and turned away, Gary cautiously raised his head and had a brief but clear view of the man's profile in the moonlight. The next moment he was back in the car, which promptly started up and bumped away over the uneven ground. By the time the twins emerged from their cover, all that remained was the imprint of tyres and two cigarette-ends ground into the grass.

Gary stirred one of them thoughtfully with his shoe. 'I've seen that bloke before,' he said. 'Don't know his name but I'm sure he's a customer.'

Rob pursed his lips in a whistle. 'Lucky he didn't see us, then. What do you reckon was going on?'

'Something they don't want Customs to know about. Which, bro, when I track down who the bloke is, could turn out to be a nice little earner.' He grinned, putting his hand on his brother's shoulder as they turned back into the trees. 'Didn't I say it was our lucky night?'

The White twins were not, after all, the only ones to notice the plane. By the following Monday, Shillingham police had received several complaints about low-flying aircraft and a farmer had reported the churning up of one of his fields as if by heavy wheels.

Nor was it the first time such complaints had been received. Three or four times a year low-flying aircraft were reported over various parts of Broadshire which neither the police nor Air Traffic Control had been able to account for.

John Baker, a uniformed inspector, was grumbling about it over coffee in the canteen. The last thing he needed on a Monday morning was a recurrent problem like this. 'God knows what they're up to; every time it happens we send someone to investigate, and every time we come up with damn-all. Short of shooting the things down, what are we supposed to do about it?'

'And they're always in different areas?' asked DI Crombie, taking another biscuit.

'Yep. Otherwise, when the moon's right, we could post watchers.'

'If they're actually landing, odds are you can take your pick between illegal immigration and drug-smuggling.'

'Quite, which is why Customs & Excise are on our backs.'

'Whereabouts was it this time?'

'On a deserted stretch between SB and Marlton. Open countryside, screened from the road by trees. Ideal situation, really.'

A couple of hours later, as Crombie was checking on a recent break-in, Baker's words suddenly came back to him. He glanced at DCI Webb, buried in his paperwork.

'This break-in on Saturday—' he began.

'Mm?'

'When reporting it, the owners also mentioned a low-flying aircraft. From what John Baker was saying, it sounds as if it landed in the same area.'

'Mm.'

'You don't think there's any connection?'

At that, Webb did look up. 'Oh come on, Alan! You're suggesting the villains laid on a private plane to remove the loot? The day that happens, I'm chucking this job in!'

Crombie grinned reluctantly. 'OK, I suppose you're right. At least the aircraft isn't our headache. Uniform are welcome to it.'

Webb nodded and returned to his papers.

CHAPTER 1

Monica Tovey, unmarried and with her fortieth birthday some years behind her, considered herself fortunate; as well she might, her life being comfortable, successful and brimful of interest. That it was also precious had never occurred to her. Until it came under threat.

Not that she recognized the threat at first; it crept stealthily up on her one mild May night, moments after she'd laid aside her book, switched off the light and settled herself for sleep.

Her mind still on the chapter she'd just finished, she was lying on the edge of sleep, drowsily watching the curtains moving in the night air. And it was then, through the open window, that she heard the sputtering sound of a car engine in trouble. The noise carried clearly in the stillness, coming steadily closer until, surely directly outside the house, it gave a final cough and choked into silence.

Monica lay listening as the driver tried repeatedly to restart the car, his increasingly frustrated attempts resulting only in a strained rumble which each time died uselessly away. Curious, she swung her legs to the floor and walked to the window, drawing the curtain aside. Immediately outside and directly beneath the street lamp stood an extraordinarily shabby van. Its driver was now standing on the pavement looking helplessly about him.

Out of petrol, no doubt. Idly, Monica wondered where the nearest all-night garage was. The one down the hill would be closed this time of night. The driver, possibly following the same line of thought, glanced at his watch. Then, drawn perhaps by the force of her gaze, he turned and stared directly up at her. Embarrassed to be caught watching, she drew hastily back, letting the curtain fall. A moment later she heard the sound of footsteps, and when cautiously she peered out again, the man had gone and the van stood alone and deserted under the street lamp. Not, Monica reflected, studying it, the kind of vehicle one expected to see in this neighbourhood. She hoped the owner'd soon remove it.

The little drama over and the night breeze cool on her body, she returned to her warm bed and promptly fell asleep.

Eight hours later, Monica woke slowly in a room now full of sunlight, and as always her first thought was to establish the day of the week. Each had a different shape to it, and until she'd moulded her thoughts to fit that which lay ahead she was oddly disoriented.

Tuesday, she remembered now. And as the key word registered, her brain obligingly slipped into gear: the Gucci rep at ten, lunch with a new buyer, Court in the afternoon, dinner with the family.

A tap on the door heralded her morning tea and she stretched luxuriously, ready for the day to begin. The housekeeper set down a tray and went to draw back the curtains. 'Another lovely morning, Miss Tovey.'

'So I see. Is there by any chance a van outside?'

'Yes, there is—a shabby-looking thing. I wonder where it came from?'

'It arrived huffing and puffing about midnight.' She sat up and pulled the pillows behind her back. 'Did my mother have a good night?'

'Yes, Miss Tovey, she slept right through.'

The new pills must be working, then; which, thank God, meant breakfast needn't be devoted to discussing alternatives. In the last months she'd begun to dread the frequent sentences which began, 'Darling, I know I'm a terrible nuisance, but—'

Monica sighed, pouring out her tea. The fact was that Maude Tovey, a prettily helpless woman who'd been cosseted by her husband for fifty years, had, on his death a year ago, transferred her total dependence to her elder daughter. It was a burden which, though she loved her mother, Monica found difficulty in shouldering.

She sipped the hot tea reflectively. A little support from Eloise would be welcome, but her sister, comfortably installed in her own home, was unwilling to interrupt her social round for less interesting duties. In any case, pandered to by a devoted husband and two sons, she was set to follow her mother's example, affecting helplessness where Monica suspected it did not exist. Regular invitations to dinner, of which tonight's was an example, eased her comfortably compliant conscience on the matter.

Still, this was no time to brood on such things. Monica hastily finished her tea and went to run her bath.

Thirty minutes later, crisply elegant in navy linen, she entered her mother's room and bent to kiss her cheek, marvelling as she always did at its softness.

'I hear you had a good night,' she said bracingly.

'Yes, thank you, dear. Such a relief.'

'You didn't hear the van, then? I was afraid it might wake you.'

'What van was that?'

'Oh, a disreputable old thing. It broke down outside in the middle of the night, and it's still there.'

'A tradesman's van, do you mean?'

'I suppose so, though there's no name on the side; and unless it goes in for overnight deliveries I can't think what it was doing out at that time. No doubt someone will arrive any minute with a can of petrol and drive it away.'

She walked to the window where the small round table was already laid. This practice of breakfasting together, she at the window table, her mother in bed, had developed since her father's death. And though it meant forfeiting her precious fifteen minutes downstairs with the paper, Monica didn't grudge her mother this short interval before she left for work.

Ignoring the van, she stood for a moment gazing at the park across the road, where early-morning walkers were already exercising their dogs. It was early summer, trees and shrubs were blossoming, and she felt an instinctive lifting of her spirits. Life was good indeed.

Preceded by a tap on the door, Mrs Bedale bustled in with the breakfast tray: grapefruit, coffee and toast for Monica; tea, bread and butter and soft-boiled egg for her mother.

'What have you on today?' Monica inquired, extracting a segment of grapefruit.

'Quite a full programme as usual,' Maude said complacently. 'Coffee at Florence's, bridge at the club this afternoon, and, of course, dinner with Eloise.'

A day as busy as her own, even if more sociably inclined. Her mother's full engagement diary had been a lifesaver over the past year.

The sound of a passing car made Monica glance outside, and she smiled. 'Gerry Ridingdale's just passed the van in his Rover. I could see the curl of his lip from here!' She folded her napkin. 'I must be on my way.'

'Will George be there this evening?'

'Undoubtedly.' Cutting off further comment, Monica kissed her mother goodbye and hurried from the room.

Of course he would, she thought, fishing the car keys from her handbag as she ran down the stairs. Eloise punctiliously included George in her invitations, as though they were already married. Which, Monica allowed, letting herself out of the rear hall door, was fair enough. It had been understood for years that when—or, she sometimes thought wryly, *if* —George's mother died, they would come together. So why did she resent rather than appreciate her sister's thoughtfulness? Perhaps, she acknowledged with sudden searing honesty, because George suffered in comparison with Justin. Which was a line of thought it was better not to pursue.

The gardens behind the Georgian terrace were long and fairly narrow, but skilful landscaping had given the Toveys' an illusion of space. Dew still lay heavy on the grass and Monica kept to the paving stones as she walked to the wooden door in the high brick wall. Behind it lay the converted mews which served the houses as garages, and by the time she let herself through the door and locked it behind her, she had disciplined her thoughts away from the family and was already anticipating the working day ahead.

'Waste of good food, that's what I call it,' Doris Trubshaw grumbled as she scraped the dried-up food off the plates into the bin. 'And they needn't think I'll knock anything off 'cos they weren't here to eat it, neither.'

'I can't think where they've got to,' her husband said anxiously. 'They never said nothing about staying out all night.' It was he who, when their lodgers hadn't appeared for breakfast, had gone to their room to find it empty and the beds unslept in.

'Probably went to a party or something.'

'Even so, they should be back by now.'

'All-night parties end with breakfast, so I've heard,' Doris said disapprovingly. 'Not that I hold with that kind of thing. Asking for trouble, if you ask me.'

'Well, I suppose you're only young once.'

His wife pursed her lips and did not reply. Though she accepted Sid's soft spot for the boys, which came of having none of their own, she didn't altogether trust her lodgers. There had been times when, while dusting their room, she'd noticed bulky newspaper parcels hidden under the beds. And once, when her Hoover nudged not altogether accidentally against one, she'd caught the gleam of silver.

Well, she wasn't one to ask questions and it was no business of hers. Nor, in view of his liking for the twins, had she mentioned it to Sid. Nevertheless, she was guarded in her dealings with the pair and determinedly strove to keep things on a business footing.

Sid, on the other hand, was delighted when they started calling him 'Pop' and taking him along to matches when Shillingham played at home. At least, Doris reflected now, his presence kept them out of trouble; they'd been involved in brawls at the ground more than once. Football was all they could talk about, and Sid was as bad when he was with them. It got on her nerves sometimes.

'They'll probably go straight to work now,' he added, looking at the clock on the wall.

'They can't, can they? Their ladders are still out the back.'

'Well then, since they'll have to look in anyway, it mightn't hurt to fry 'em a rasher or two, eh, love? They'll need something inside them to start the day.'

Doris threw him one of her looks and, picking up the Hoover, pointedly left the room.

Randall Tovey's was arguably the best known fashion store in Broadshire. Founded by Monica's grandfather during the First World War, it had started life as a small dress shop in Duke Street catering for the fashion-conscious middle classes. Tovey himself had been a quiet, unassuming man, and while proud of his brainchild and its success, he was content with the small niche it occupied and had no plans to expand it.

His son, however, was of a different mould. Innovative and ambitious, his acute business brain saw possibilities which Randall had never dreamed of. At first his father tried to put brakes on his schemes, alarmed at the apparent risks Humphrey was taking. But gradually, as the plans took effect and the small shop began to flourish as never before, he relaxed and gave the boy his head.

He never regretted it. Under Humphrey's direction they moved to new premises in East Parade, Shillingham's premier shopping area, at the same time dropping the cheaper lines to which, by way of insurance, Randall had clung, and stocking designer clothes from Paris and Rome as well as the better British houses.

The store was Humphrey's life, and one of his great disappointments was that he had no sons to follow him. He tended to judge all females by his wife, whom he adored but who had no business sense whatever. None the less, her slim figure and unerring sense of fashion were in themselves good advertisements, and, having assumed his daughters would also be mere showcases, he was disconcerted rather than otherwise when Monica announced her intention of joining the firm.

Nor was it a passing fancy. He'd been first touched and then astounded by her determination to prove herself, studying fashion design and buying techniques with passionate intensity, taking business management courses and giving up her evenings to night-school while Eloise danced and flirted her way through her teens.

Humphrey'd been aware, though, that no amount of dedication would make up for that instinctive eye for style which was an essential requirement, and when his daughter displayed this in full measure, his relief was profound. Monica had as many new ideas to put before him as he'd had for his own father. At her instigation they diversified into luxury lingerie, then model hats, shoes, belts and handbags, so that an entire outfit might be purchased at the same time. The fame and prestige of the store grew steadily, achieving an eminence undreamed of by its founder, and by the time of Humphrey's own death the previous year it had become one of the leading fashion stores in the country.

Nor did it suffer the indignity of having its name abbreviated; the complacent remark, 'I bought it at Randall Tovey's,' was as much an indication of the buyer's standing as that of the store.

An integral part of the firm was Miss Hermione Tulip. Now in her seventies, she was a familiar figure with her well-cut silver hair and heavily applied make-up. Tall, thin, extremely elegant and unvaryingly dressed in black, she had an unerring eye for personal style, and there were many who refused to buy an outfit without her approval.

That morning she was, as always, awaiting Monica's arrival in the central foyer of the store. This was both the heart of the building and the prospective buyer's first glimpse of it, and much thought had been given to its ambience. Logs burned throughout the winter in its fireplace, and now a massive vase of lilacs screened the grate. And here, perhaps most important of all, was Miss Tulip's desk, so that she was on hand to offer a personal welcome to each caller.

'The Duchess's secretary telephoned,' she reported now, handing Monica her mail. 'Lady Henrietta's wedding date has been fixed, and Her Grace would like a few outfits sent to Beckworth House to chose from.'

'Well, you know her size, Tulie,' Monica said absently, flicking through the envelopes. 'May I leave it to you?'

'Of course. And though nothing was mentioned for Her Ladyship, I thought we might send up the de Franzi wedding gown, too. It would suit her admirably.'

'By all means.'

It was 9.20, ten minutes before the doors opened to the public, and from the tea-room behind the ivy-twined columns came the smell of freshly ground coffee. Anticipating her own cup, Monica walked up the wide, shallow staircase to her office.

Abbie Marlow was seated at the kitchen table, chin in hand, watching her mother tossing the salad for their lunch. She'd been excused school this week in order to revise for her O-levels and had wandered down from her room in search of sustenance.

'How's it going?' Claudia asked, setting the large wooden bowl on the table.

Abbie pulled a face. 'Bor-ing. After next month, I'll never open another history book as long as I live! I hope you're impressed by my willpower,' she added, pulling the bowl towards her and ladling salad on to her plate. 'For two pins I'd ditch the lot and go out and play tennis.'

'I'm most impressed, but it will be worth it in the long run.'

'But I need an incentive *now*,' Abbie said, 'a reward for all the slogging.' She brightened. 'How about the cinema this evening—something to look forward to?'

'Oh, darling, I can't; we're going to the Teals' for dinner. I thought I told you.'

'Oh yes. Well, never mind, I'll phone Mandy.' She licked

some vinaigrette off her finger. 'Don't you ever feel awkward, spending so much time with the Teals?'

'Awkward?' Claudia repeated blankly.

'Well, she was engaged to Daddy once, wasn't she?'

'Good heavens, that was years ago—before I even met him.'

'All the same, I know *I* wouldn't like to be always hob-nobbing with my husband's ex.'

'But that's not how I think of Eloise. She's my friend as much as Daddy's.'

Abbie shrugged, conceding the point. 'Any news of Theo?' she asked casually.

Her mother hid a smile. 'Not lately.'

'I wonder if they'll be having a garden party again this summer. If they do, wangle me an invite, won't you?'

'I'll do what I can; but he's a sophisticated young man, darling. You'd be better with someone nearer your own age.'

'Meaning he won't notice me any more than he did last year?'

'I didn't say that.'

'Oh well, I can dream, can't I?' She put down her knife and fork. 'Back to the grindstone. Thanks for lunch.' And she was gone.

But Claudia sat for several minutes, turning the pepper mill in her fingers. She'd almost forgotten Harry was once engaged to Eloise. *Did* he ever have regrets? Or did she? It was a thought that hadn't occurred to her in twenty years, and she found it disturbing.

CHAPTER 2

During her busy day Monica had forgotten about the broken-down van, and was surprised on arriving home to find it still outside the house. She perforce drew up behind it and got out of the car, frowning. From its appearance, no one had been near it all day. She jotted down its registration number, and as soon as she entered the house, phoned the police station at the top of the hill.

'Sergeant Penrose? It's Miss Tovey. Do you know anything about a van that's broken down outside our house? . . . It arrived in the middle of the night. The driver tried to restart it, failed, and walked off. I assumed he'd gone to a garage for help . . . Yes, it's most annoying, especially since we're going out this evening and I need to park in front of the house. As it is, I've had to take next door's space . . . Yes, I made a note of it.' She read out the registration number, nodding as he repeated it back to her. 'That's right. Would you? Thank you so much.'

She replaced the phone and put her head round the drawing-room door. Her mother was relaxing on the sofa with her feet up.

'Hello, darling. Had a good day?'

'A busy one. Hasn't anyone been to see about that van?'

'Not that I know of. Margaret remarked on it when she brought me back from bridge. It's a disgrace to the neighbourhood.'

'Well, I've phoned Sergeant Penrose, so I hope he'll take care of it. I'm going up for a bath. Shan't be long.'

Officially, an abandoned vehicle was a matter for the local council, which Penrose bet Miss Tovey knew quite well. However, since she was a senior magistrate and personally inconvenienced, he didn't mind looking into it. He'd not much on at the moment, anyway; North Park was a wealthy, law-abiding suburb, and while a posting there was regarded as a cushy number, the main drawback was boredom. He therefore began by checking the police national computer, and moments later had ascertained there were no reports either of the van being stolen or any interest having been expressed in it.

The last registered owner was named as Gary White, 24 Trafalgar Street. Not the most salubrious part of town, Penrose reflected. Well, he'd go and look at the van, at least;

it was a nice evening for a stroll. But that, for the moment, was as far as he could go. Magistrate or not, it was too soon to go chasing after the owner. He was probably planning to come back for it after work.

'I'm going to check on an abandoned vehicle,' he told his colleague. And by the time he got back it would be the end of his shift and he could go home.

Monica saw Penrose arrive from her bedroom window as she was dressing for the dinner-party. He circled the van a couple of times, tapping the tyres, checking the number-plates and examining the bodywork. He also peered through the dirty rear window, and studied the rack on the roof. Then, after making some notes in his pocket-book, he turned and walked back up the hill. At least, she thought, she'd registered a complaint and with luck the van would be gone by the time they returned tonight.

She bent forward, looking critically at her reflection in the glass and hoping the outfit she'd chosen would be suitable. Eloise held different levels of dinner-party, ranging from family (plus George) to what Monica dubbed the Pulling-Out-All-Stops occasions. These were usually designed to impress either customers or suppliers of Justin's wine business, or fellow members of the Arts Appreciation Society which she and the Marlows supported so ardently.

And the trouble was, Monica thought, giving her hair a final pat, one was never advised in advance what type of company to expect. She'd tried asking, but as Eloise was deliberately vague, she no longer bothered. In any event, the food was always excellent; even for the smaller occasions a firm of caterers was employed, who took over the kitchen for the evening and left everything spotlessly tidy afterwards.

Picking up her handbag, Monica went downstairs to collect her mother.

'You're not going out *again*, George?' Ethel Latimer looked peevishly up at her son as he bent to kiss her cheek.

'Mother dear, I've not been out for weeks!'

'Just all day and every day,' she said with a sniff.

'Well, of course I go to work, but I spend the evenings with you. And Betsy will be here to keep you company.' Long-suffering Betsy, who had become almost one of the family.

'Betsy doesn't read to me like you do.'

'But she plays cards and does the crossword, doesn't she? Anyway, Tuesday's your favourite television evening.'

'I suppose you're going to see that woman,' Ethel said, unmollified.

George held on to his patience. 'If you mean Monica, yes, she'll be there.'

'I know you're both waiting for me to die, so you can marry. I'm surprised you haven't put something in my tea before this.'

'Mother, please don't be ridiculous. Nobody wants you to die. Now, have a pleasant evening. I'll look in to say good night when I get back.'

And before she could make any more complaints, he walked quickly from the room. Was he a good son, he wondered, to consider her as much as he did, or simply a weak-willed fool for allowing her to ruin his life? He was forty-eight, damn it, surely he was entitled to some life of his own? But he'd promised Father to take care of her—he couldn't just abandon her.

In the early days, any girl he'd been fond enough of to bring home had wilted under his mother's relentless disapproval and disappeared from the scene. Once, when he'd dared to become engaged, she had had a heart attack. Even now, he wondered how she'd engineered it. Still, it had the desired effect and the engagement was called off.

After that, George admitted defeat and buried himself in his work, rising steadily through the bank to a position of considerable authority. In his work environment at least he was highly thought of, his decisions respected and his opinions sought. It was a Jekyll and Hyde existence, but his career afforded some compensation for what his personal life lacked, and the years had passed reasonably contentedly. Then, four years ago, he'd met Monica.

How did the old song go? *But it's when he thinks he's past love, Oh it's then he meets his last love, And he loves her as he's never loved before.* Well, that was how it had been—still was. And Monica, unlike her young predecessors, was not in the least intimidated by his mother. Though unfailingly polite, she played the old lady at her own game, and he discerned in his mother a grudging though well-disguised respect.

At the time they met, Mrs Latimer had been going through one of her actual rather than imagined bouts of ill health, and the doctor was doubtful of her chances of recovery. It had not seemed unreasonable to ask Monica to postpone their wedding plans, which would be sure to upset the old lady.

But with what George couldn't help regarding as typical perversity, Ethel Latimer made a complete recovery and resumed her tyrannical control over her son's home life.

Monica had been incredibly understanding. 'We're not teenagers, George,' she'd said. 'We've waited this long, a year or two more won't make any difference.' But the 'year or two' showed signs of stretching indefinitely. When Humphrey Tovey had died, George wondered briefly if the two old ladies might be company for each other, thus freeing their offspring to marry. But that hope was stillborn when they took an instant and mutual dislike to each other. Understandably, perhaps, since Maude Tovey, though not many years younger, was still an attractive and fashionable woman with a wide circle of friends. Ethel seemed decades older, with her inward-looking, sour view of life.

So he and Monica continued their long-drawn-out engagement, managing discreet weekends away now and then and generally seeing as much of each other as their busy lives allowed. Occasionally, and to his shame, George found himself resenting her patience, suspecting it meant she was not as anxious as he to marry. If that were so, he thought he understood why: he had suspected almost from the time he met her that Monica was in love with her brother-in-law.

What he was not sure of was whether she recognized the fact.

There were ten at the dinner-party. Harry and Claudia Marlow were there, George, of course, and both the Teal boys, together with Jeremy's live-in girlfriend. Monica was not impressed by the latter, whom she'd met before. A tall, willowy blonde, she had a permanently bored expression which marred her lovely face, and was given to draping herself against the furniture to display her admittedly perfect figure. Her name was Primrose, which Monica conceded was no fault of her own.

Come to that, Monica wished she could be fonder of her nephews. Outwardly they were a credit to their parents— tall, good-looking, well-groomed and with perfect manners; the sort of young men, in fact, who postured self-consciously in sportswear advertisements, accompanied by appropriately dressed females and golden retrievers. But behind their ready smiles and smooth faces, she had no idea what they were thinking. Even more uncomfortably, she didn't quite trust them.

Summoned, perhaps, by her musings, Theo came over and took the seat next to hers. 'A very elegant dress, Aunt, if I may say so. From the Spring Collections?'

She looked at him sharply but his face, as always, was bland. 'Just a little thing I ran up.'

He laughed. 'I must say it's gratifying to have such glamorous relations. Mother looks a picture, doesn't she?'

Monica acknowledged that she did. Her sister not only possessed the family dress sense in full measure, she had the knack of investing any garment she wore with her own stamp, just as her large, horn-rimmed spectacles had over the years become a personal fashion accessory. Taller and fairer than Monica, she wore her silver-blonde hair in a sleek, chin-length bob which perfectly complimented her oval face and round grey eyes. Tonight the green chiffon dress she wore, swathed over narrow hips, needed only the simplest gold chain by way of adornment.

Yes, they were a good-looking family, Monica thought complacently. It was no wonder Justin preferred to entertain customers at home. Yet, even with the backing of her catering team, there were times when Eloise was not prepared to play hostess. Monica tried not to doubt the veracity of the migraines which frequently laid her low when less interesting guests were due. On such occasions Justin had no course but to resort to restaurants, and not infrequently invited herself to be his hostess. Her fluency in French and Italian, painstakingly perfected to ease her way at the Collections, was a particular asset with his continental suppliers.

Monica watched her sister chatting animatedly with Harry Marlow. She really didn't see why she should feel embarrassed when they were together, since obviously neither they nor their spouses did. Their former engagement was, after all, ancient history, and both marriages seemed happy enough.

Deliberately combating that embarrassment, Monica studied Harry as he stood with his head bent attentively to her sister. Unlike Justin, whose hair was now steel grey, and George, with his rapidly fading thatch, Harry's was still dark, and if his jawline had thickened over the years, it served only to give him a more authoritative air. All in all, the years had been kind to him and he was still a very attractive man. Small wonder that Eloise, who thrived on masculine attention, liked to keep him around her.

Dinner was announced, and served as always by one of the trio of caterers. Two young men and a girl, they worked democratically, taking it in turns to cook, wash up and wait at table. This evening it was the darker man, immaculate in white dinner jacket. Monica noted drily that Primrose's eyes fluttered towards him more than once.

Justin, on her right at the head of the table, claimed her attention. 'How was Court this afternoon?' He was a fellow magistrate and occasionally they sat on the same bench.

'Pretty run-of-the-mill. At least we're spared football hooligans, now the season's over.' She smiled. 'Actually, being a JP does have its advantages. I unashamedly pulled strings this evening in an attempt to get an old van removed from our doorway.'

Justin paused, his fork half way to his mouth. 'Really? Who does it belong to?'

'I wish I knew. It broke down in the middle of the night and no one's collected it yet. I'm hoping Sergeant Penrose will do the necessary.'

'Perhaps it was deliberately dumped,' George suggested.

'I don't think so. I heard it arrive, coughing and spluttering. The driver tried several times to restart it.'

'Well, if it was only last night, you haven't given him long to get organized.'

'True. I probably wouldn't have made such a fuss if it hadn't been so unsightly.'

Jeremy, on her left, turned towards her. 'What is it you've been making a fuss about, *ma tante*?'

'A dirty van outside our house.'

Her mother took up the story. 'Yes, it's perfectly disgraceful. I don't know what our neighbours must think. Monica heard it arrive during the night—she was afraid it might have wakened me, but these new sleeping pills proved their worth, I'm glad to say.'

Theo, on his grandmother's far side, leaned round her. 'A dirty van sullying North Park Drive? The very idea! Have it towed away at once!'

'I'm trying to,' Monica said evenly, regretting by now that she had broached the subject.

'Hasn't it got a name on the side?' George again.

'Obviously not, or I'd have contacted whoever's responsible. It's simply a dirty green van with some kind of rack on the roof.'

There was a moment of complete silence, which for some reason made her uncomfortable. Perhaps it was her tone of voice which had surprised them. She said with a forced laugh, 'I know this is a fascinating topic of conversation, but can we move on to something else?'

There was a brief, uncertain pause. Then Claudia said

valiantly, 'I hope you're all coming to the Private View next week?'

'What is it this time?'

After a shaky start general conversation resumed and Monica felt herself relax. She looked up to find George watching her and, catching her eye, he gave her an encouraging smile. Dear George, she thought, smiling back; he'd forgiven her her snappy rejoinder. She felt a rush of warmth for him, mingled as usual with an indeterminate sense of guilt. Pushing both aside, she directed her attention to her cooling meal.

The van was still there when they arrived home, the light from the street lamp waking no reflections in its grimy surface. Monica dropped her mother at the door and drove round to the mews to garage the car. So much for her attempt at string-pulling, she thought wryly, and with a mental shrug resolved to let the matter take its course.

Later, however, on the point of sleep, the van driver's face came into her mind, white under the street lamp and staring straight up at her. Unaccountably she shivered and, pulling the bedclothes more tightly round her, she turned on her side and determinedly settled to sleep.

Doris Trubshaw stirred, felt the space on the mattress beside her, and heaved herself up on one elbow. Her husband was at the window again, holding the curtain aside and peering into the street below.

'Come back to bed, love,' she said gently.

'I thought I heard the van.'

'Well, they've got their own key.'

'It wasn't them, anyway. I can't think where they've got to. They've never done this before.'

Her heart contracted at the sight of his drooping shoulders, the sparse hair ruffled from an uneasy sleep. 'They'll come back when they're good and ready. They can take care of theirselves, them two, don't you fret.'

'But we're responsible for them in a way.'

'That we're not!' Her voice had sharpened. 'They've been up to all sorts of tricks I've not bothered you with, but if one has backfired they've only themselves to blame.'

Sid, on the point of climbing back into bed, stopped and stared at her. 'What are you on about? What tricks?'

'Least said, soonest mended.'

'Doris, for pity's sake! What have they been up to?'

'A spot of burglary, I'd say. Suspicious packages under their beds—that kind of thing.'

'But—why didn't you tell me?'

'Because I knew you'd worry and it's not our problem. Can't take on the cares of the world, you know.'

Carefully he eased himself into the bed beside her, sliding as he always did into the hollow in the middle. She felt his feet, cold from his sojourn at the window, brush against her warm ones. 'I wish you'd told me,' he said flatly.

'And what good would that have done? It's not as if they're our own. As long as they keep their room tidy and pay the rent, we can't interfere. Or would you have gone to the police?' she added mockingly.

'No, of course not.' He sounded shocked, missing the sarcasm in her voice. 'But I could have warned them, like. Told them it doesn't pay in the long run.'

She gave a mirthless laugh. 'But it probably does. Better than their window-cleaning, anyway. How d'you think they could afford those leather jackets?'

He gave a little shiver and she leaned over to tuck the blanket more tightly round his shoulders. 'Go to sleep, love. There might be some news in the morning.'

But there wasn't, and at midday Sid could stand it no longer. Miserable and anxious, he made his reluctant way to Carrington Street police station.

'Yes, sir? Can I help you?' The desk sergeant hadn't looked up from his papers.

Sid cleared his throat. 'I'd—I'd like to report two missing persons.'

'Two? Don't do things by halves, do you?' Fenton looked

up quizzically, regretting his flippancy when he saw the man's drawn face. 'Right, sir, who are you missing?'

'Our lodgers. Two lads by the name of White. Brothers. They went out after supper on Monday, and we've heard nothing since.'

'A moonlight flit?'

'No, their rent's paid up and everything's still in their room.' Even the prized leather jackets.

'And you are?'

'Mr Trubshaw, twenty-four Trafalgar Street.'

Fenton looked up, frowning. The address sounded familiar and almost at once slotted into place. Jim Penrose and the abandoned van Miss Tovey'd reported. Best tread carefully here.

'And the two lads are called White, you say. Christian names?'

'Gary and Rob. Robert.'

That definitely struck a chord, a more longstanding one. 'Did they have any form of transport, sir?'

'Aye, a van. They're window-cleaners, like.'

'Could you describe it?'

'Well, it's not up to much. Dark green Ford Escort. Can't recall the registration offhand.'

'Any distinguishing features?'

'Only the rack on top, for the ladders.'

Something in the sergeant's manner sharpened Sid's apprehension. 'You've heard something, haven't you?'

'It's possible we might have something on the van. One answering to this description was abandoned in North Park on Monday night.'

'Abandoned?' Sid stared at him. 'Then where are the lads?'

'I couldn't say, sir.'

'No.' The old man shook his head positively. 'It can't be theirs, not in North Park. They never go up there.'

'Might have been on their way back from somewhere and run out of juice.'

'Then where *are* they? It's nearly two days ago!'

Fenton regarded the agitated little man. His concern seemed genuine, and it wasn't motivated by self-interest since the boys didn't owe him money. He wondered how much he knew about his lodgers' activities. Might be worth checking to see if he had form himself. Not, he reminded himself, that they'd been able to pin much on the White twins other than causing a disturbance at football matches. Too fly by half, that pair.

'Thank you for reporting the matter, sir,' he said formally. 'We'll keep you informed.'

It was lunch-time again, and once more Claudia and Abbie sat at the kitchen table. It was their first meeting of the day; Claudia'd had an early breakfast before leaving for a dental appointment.

'How was the dinner-party?' Abbie asked.

'All right.'

'No need to rave about it!'

'Actually, I didn't enjoy it as much as usual. I don't know why.' She did, though. After her daughter's comment yesterday, she'd paid more attention to Eloise and her husband, and what she'd seen made her faintly uneasy. Which, after all these years, was ridiculous. *Damn* Abbie for sowing doubts in her mind.

'Was Theo there?'

Claudia dragged her attention back. 'Yes, and Jeremy and Primrose.'

'Oh, *Primrose*!' said Abbie with scorn. 'Poseuse supreme!' She took a mouthful of spaghetti. 'Who else?'

'Only the Toveys and George.'

'The usual gang, in fact. What did you eat?'

'Salmon and garlic mousse, veal cutlets and a kind of bombe thing.'

'Good?'

'Yes, delicious. Perhaps I just wasn't in the mood. How was the cinema?'

Abbie launched into a description of the film she'd seen the previous evening, and Claudia's thoughts wandered again. What exactly did she know of Harry and Eloise's past connection? Simply that they'd met at the tennis club when Eloise was still at Ashbourne, and become engaged on her eighteenth birthday. Then, some months later, she'd met Justin—through Monica, Claudia seemed to remember. And, as Harry himself had told her, Eloise lost her head over him. 'After all,' she remembered him adding caustically, 'the Teals *are* one of Shillingham's oldest families.'

So the engagement was off and within a month or two Eloise married Justin. It was more than two years later that Claudia's family moved to Shillingham—too long, surely, for any suspicion that he'd turned to her on the rebound.

The fact that they were still so friendly with the Teals had bothered her not all. She and Eloise had similar interests, particularly in the art field, and spent a considerable time together without their husbands. It was not only foolish but dangerous to put all that in jeopardy because of a chance remark by her daughter.

'Actually,' Claudia said suddenly, interrupting Abbie's narrative, 'it *was* a pleasant evening, and I enjoyed it.'

Abbie looked at her in surprise. 'That's good,' she said.

Sergeant Penrose had been advised of Mr Trubshaw's visit and was waiting by the van when the CID car arrived and the two detectives got out.

Bob Dawson walked round it critically. 'Owners never heard of a wash leather, by the look of it. Have you tried the doors?'

'No call to,' Penrose reminded him. 'It's not been here forty-eight hours yet. I only came earlier as a favour to Miss Tovey.'

'Well, as you'll have gathered, now that the owners are reported missing we're stepping things up.' He peered through the nearside window. 'Keys in the ignition, would you believe! In any other area it would have been nicked before now and saved us all this bother!' He wrapped a handkerchief round his hand and tried the handle. The door opened. Dawson stuck his head inside, then withdrew quickly. 'Oi, oi. Something not quite kosher here.'

'How d'you mean, Skipper?' DC Cummings made to bend forward but Dawson gestured him away. 'Use your handkerchief, Steve, and see if the rear doors are unlocked.'

They were. On the floor of the van lay a heap of stained tarpaulin. The two sergeants exchanged glances.

'Thinking what I'm thinking, Jim?'

Penrose had paled. 'Afraid so.'

Dawson felt in his pocket and took out a pencil. Leaning inside the van, he used it to lift a corner of the tarpaulin and flick it aside. Then he stood back with a deep sigh. Now exposed to view lay the bodies of two identical young men with short blond hair, wearing the green tracksuits of Shillingham United.

'Well, well, well,' he said, feeling in vain for first one pulse, then the other. 'So they've gone to the big football ground in the sky.'

Cummings, who'd turned hastily away as the bodies were uncovered, managed to find his voice. 'You—you know who they are, Skip?'

'Certainly I do; our paths have crossed more than once. It's the White twins, lad, better known on the terraces as the Lily-White Boys.'

CHAPTER 3

By the time DCI Webb and Sergeant Jackson arrived, uniform officers were posted at strategic points on the pavement and the van was screened from public gaze. Though for all the interest the public was showing, the precautions hardly seemed necessary. North Park residents had been brought up to disregard that which was none of their business, a tendency which boded ill in a murder inquiry.

Dawson, Cummings and Penrose were awaiting them on

the pavement, together with the Coroner's Officer, a police constable called Smithers.

'So what have we got this time?' Webb asked, as Cummings opened the car door for him.

It was Dawson who answered. 'Two for the price of one, Guv; the White twins. "In their death they were not divided," as you might say.'

'Very pretty. I gather you made the ID.'

'That's right, I've had several dealings with them. Football mad, they were, and not averse to a bit of a punch-up at the ground now and then.'

Webb and Jackson exchanged a glance. It was the opinion at Carrington Street that Bob himself was 'football mad', and according to his colleagues the only time he showed any animation was at a United match.

'We'd our suspicions on several breaking and entering jobs, too,' Dawson was continuing, 'but we couldn't make any stick.'

'Right.' Webb turned to Smithers. 'Get on to Dr Stapleton, will you, Brian, and the undertakers. Has the police surgeon seen them?'

'Yes, as luck would have it he was driving past, so he stopped and did the necessary.'

'I'd better go and have a look.' Webb moved cautiously inside the screen, stepping over the equipment which lay in the road. The senior Scene of Crime man looked up with a grimace. 'I don't know about you, Dave, but give me the winter any time. This warm weather does nothing for my job satisfaction.'

Webb's throat closed in sympathy. 'I see what you mean. So what's the gen?'

'Prepare for a double take—it's uncanny how alike they are. Gave me quite a turn, I can tell you, seeing them side by side like that.'

Webb moved forward and glanced inside the van. The two young men lay on their backs like broken dolls, covered from the waist down in dirty tarpaulin. Their heads were turned slightly towards each other, and as Dick Hodges had said it was like looking at the same person twice. Everything about them was identical, not only the style and colour of their hair but the way it grew, the neat ears set close against their heads, the full, rather childish mouths, each with a small mole at the left-hand corner; and, of course, the identical green tracksuits which were the training uniform of Shillingham United. And it was here that the sole distinguishing feature could be seen: the sweatshirt of the twin on the right had a jagged tear which was caked with dark blood and surrounded by a swarm of flies.

Webb stood looking down on the bodies, filled with an angry sadness. They looked so *young*. Whatever their lives had been, it was a tragic waste that they'd ended so soon.

'We've finished the photos and fingerprinting,' Hodges said, breaking the silence. 'Trouble is, since they were dead when they were dumped in there, we haven't got a scene to work on.'

'Doc Pringle have any comments?'

'Without moving them he couldn't tell much. As you see, only one of them has an obvious wound, but the other could have got it in the back.'

'At least time of death shouldn't pose too many problems; they left their lodgings "after supper" on Monday and according to the report the van was dumped here around midnight.'

'That makes sense—rigor mortis has worn off. If we can establish the time of that last meal, the stomach contents should clinch it.'

The sound of a car drawing up and voices beyond the screen alerted them to the arrival of the pathologist, and Webb went out to greet him.

'You were lucky to catch me,' Dr Stapleton said tersely. 'I was on my way to a lecture.'

He was a thin-faced man with sparse hair and an unbending manner. Even in the warm sunshine he gave an impression of coldness. Too much preoccupation with death, Jackson reflected, watching him talk to Smithers and the Governor. Then Stapleton disappeared behind the screens and Webb turned to Penrose, jerking his head towards the houses behind them.

'One of the residents reported the van, right?'

'Yes, sir. Number five.'

Webb turned and surveyed the handsome terrace of houses. There were nine in all, each with an imposing flight of steps leading up to a portico and, along the pavement, a stretch of railings tipped with gold paint which screened off a basement area. The façades were smooth stucco uniformly painted cream, the sash windows typically Georgian.

'Very tasteful,' he said. 'Has no one been out to inquire what we're up to?'

'No, sir.'

'Not even the woman who complained about the van?'

'That was Miss Tovey, sir, of Randall Tovey. You know, the JP. I suppose she'll be at the shop.'

'Well, I'll try knocking on her door and see what we come up with.'

The woman who answered his knock was middle-aged, pleasant-faced, and wore her hair in an old-fashioned bun.

'Good afternoon, ma'am. Is this Miss Tovey's house?'

Her eyes had gone beyond him to the activity round the shrouded van. With an effort she brought them back to his face.

'She lives here, yes, sir.'

'Is she at home?'

'Not at the moment.'

'Anyone in apart from yourself?'

'No, sir; Mrs Tovey's gone to her bowls.'

'Know anything about this van out here?'

Her eyes slid back to it. 'Miss Tovey mentioned it yesterday morning. She heard it come during the night.'

'Have you noticed anyone near it?'

'Me? Her eyes widened. 'No, sir.'

'Where is Miss Tovey, do you know?'

'She'll be at the store till five-thirty.'

It was just after three. Better to see her straight away.

The woman said uncertainly, 'Is something wrong, sir?'

'Nothing, I imagine, that will concern Miss Tovey.' And with a smile to conceal his prevarication, Webb turned and went back down the steps to the waiting policemen.

'Bob, I'd like you and Steve here to get over to Randall Tovey's. Have a word with Miss Tovey and find out all you can about the arrival of the van.' He turned to Penrose. 'You took her phone call, didn't you? Did she mention the driver?'

'Yes, sir. Said he tried several times to start the engine, then walked off down the hill. She thought he'd gone for petrol.'

'Let's hope she got a good look at him,' Webb said grimly. 'Right, Mr Penrose, if the press arrive before you leave with the deceased, tell them we're preparing a release and there'll be a press conference at noon tomorrow. I should be back from the post-mortem by then.' He signalled to Jackson and climbed back into the car. 'Meanwhile,' he added, fastening his seat-belt, 'we'll look in at the victims' address and see if their landlady knows anything. Trafalgar Street, isn't it?'

'That's the one, Guv.'

As they were driving down the hill a car came screeching past them and swerved into the parking place they'd just vacated.

'And here's the press, right on cue,' Jackson grinned. 'Trust Bill Hardy to be first on the scene.'

'He's less time than the dailies, remember. Not that he'll get much for tonight's edition; we haven't much ourselves.'

Trafalgar Street was one of a maze of roads lying to the east of Station Road, most of them named after famous British victories. Trafalgar itself was the first turning past the station and possessed what must have been an added attraction to its recently departed residents: it was immediately adjacent to the football ground.

The door of No. 24 opened as they stopped the car, revealing a small, worried-looking man. 'Is there any news?' he blurted out, as Webb started up the path.

'Mr—?'

'Trubshaw. I been down to the station this morning, I—'

'Yes,' Webb said gently, 'I know. Perhaps we could come in for a minute?'

As he stepped into the small hallway, Jackson close behind him, a woman appeared at the kitchen door.

'The wife,' Trubshaw muttered unnecessarily. Webb nodded to her and she followed them into the living-room.

Webb introduced himself and Jackson. 'I believe Gary and Robert White had lodgings with you?' he began formally.

'Yes?'

'Could you tell me the last time you saw them?'

'Monday evening, like I told the other copper. We all had supper as usual and later on they went out.'

Webb turned to the woman. She was standing in the doorway watching him closely, and he had the fanciful idea that she was there to protect her husband. 'What time was your meal, Mrs Trubshaw?'

'Half-six, as usual.'

'What did you serve?'

She raised her eyebrows, and for a moment Webb feared he might have to explain why he needed this information. But then she said, 'Cottage pie. Same as always on Mondays.'

'And you finished eating at what time?'

'Seven, seven-fifteen.'

'Then the Whites went out?'

'Not immediately, no. They watched a couple of TV programmes, but they were restless. I remember thinking they were strung up about something.'

'Restless in what way?'

'Kept fidgeting and looking at their watches. And come to think of it, they didn't eat as much as usual.'

'Did they mention what they were going to do that evening?'

She shook her head. 'They never say.'

'Well, we never ask, do we?' Trubshaw put in defensively.

'I know they often meet their mates, either at the Whistle Stop or the clubhouse.'

'The football club?'

'That's right.'

'So what time did they go out?'

'Must have been getting on for nine.'

Mrs Trubshaw said suddenly, 'You know something, don't you? Something you're not telling us.'

'I'm afraid so, yes. The Whites are dead, Mrs Trubshaw. I'm sorry.'

'What—both of them?' The man was staring at him, suddenly trembling. His wife moved swiftly to his side.

'How?' she asked baldly.

'We're not sure yet.'

'But they didn't crash the van. We were told it had been dumped.'

'Where—' Trubshaw broke off, cleared his throat and tried again. 'Where were they found?'

Webb hesitated, but they'd know soon enough. 'In the back of the van.'

The Trubshaws regarded him with horror. 'They've been there all the time? Then what—I mean, how—?'

'We don't know, but we'll find out.'

Mrs Trubshaw said, 'Are you saying they were killed deliberately?'

'It looks like it, yes.'

'Oh my God!' Trubshaw sat down on the nearest chair.

'How long had they been with you?' Webb inquired. There seemed to be more than a lodger–landlord relationship, certainly with the man. A surrogate family, perhaps.

'Going on three years now.' His voice was shaking.

'Do you know anything about their family? Next of kin, and so on?'

'They never had none. Brought up in an orphanage. Only had each other—till they came here.' His eyes filled with sudden tears. 'They called me Pop,' he added brokenly. His wife laid an awkward hand on his arm.

'You're sure about that—that they'd no family?'

'That's what they told us,' the woman answered. 'Mind —not wanting to speak ill of the dead and all, but I didn't believe everything they said, not by a long chalk.'

'Doris!'

'I'm sorry, love. While they was alive I kept quiet, and maybe I did wrong. Now they're dead, nothing I say can hurt them.'

'And what are you saying, Mrs Trubshaw?' Webb asked quietly.

'Well—' She averted her eyes from her husband's plead-ing, upturned face. 'I'm pretty sure they handled stolen goods, though whether they did the stealing theirselves I couldn't say. Several times I noticed things in their room, pushed out of sight but not properly hid. But Sid was that soft about them, I kept it to myself.'

So Bob Dawson's suspicions were justified. 'What kind of things did you see?'

'I didn't look too close, but silver—stuff like that. And once, early in the morning, I saw them carrying something bulky out to the van. It looked like one of them videos.'

'I see. Well, some officers will be along later to examine their room. If you've a key, perhaps it could be locked till they arrive.'

Mrs Trubshaw was affronted. 'We're responsible citizens, Officer. If you say not to go in their room, then we won't. There's no call to lock doors in this house.'

He said gently, 'Mrs Trubshaw, your husband was fond of the boys. He—'

'He won't go covering up for them, if that's what you're getting at. You'll be looking for clues to the killer, won't you? Well, I reckon Sid wants him caught even more than you do.'

Webb sighed and turned to the man, who was staring miserably into space. 'Coming back to the next of kin, Mr Trubshaw: if there's no family, we'll require you formally to identify them.'

Trubshaw gasped and blanched, and again his wife came

to his aid. 'I'll do it,' she said staunchly. 'They didn't mean as much to me.'

'Very well. Thank you. A car will collect you in an hour or so. There's no need to worry, they look quite peaceful.'

His reassurance proved unnecessary. 'I laid out both my parents,' Mrs Trubshaw told him stoutly, 'I know what to expect.'

'That's all right, then. Well now, Mr Trubshaw: you say the twins used to meet friends for drinks. Can you remember any names?'

The man gave himself a shake, trying to collect his thoughts. 'Let's see. Not surnames; I never heard those. But there was Mike and Charlie and Jango. They were in the same gang, like, though not what you'd call close. The twins weren't that close to anyone but each other.'

The names might ring a bell with Bob Dawson, Webb thought, and a warning one at that. He'd spoken of fighting at the ground.

'They belonged to a gang, did they?'

'Well—' Sid Trubshaw shuffled his feet uncomfortably. 'They was all members of the Supporters' Club, like, but a group of them usually met for a jar before matches and went along together.'

'With the aim of causing trouble?'

'I wouldn't say that.' Trubshaw looked as though he regretted volunteering the information.

'All the same, there often *was* trouble, wasn't there? Rival fans beaten up, and so on?'

'Well, high spirits sometimes get out of hand.'

Obviously a visit to the club would be necessary. Bob and Steve could see to that. As Webb took his leave of the Trubshaws, he wondered how they were getting on with Miss Tovey, JP.

Miss Tulip had experienced a moment of sheer panic when the two large figures came through the door. She'd no doubt whatever who they were; unattached males were rare at Randall Tovey's, appearing only in the weeks before Christmas to purchase expensive lingerie and handbags for their ladies. In any case these two were literally in a different class, and while they hesitated just inside the door, she made a lightning assessment of them.

The older one had dull black hair and heavy-lidded eyes under dark brows. He looked like a mournful bloodhound —which, she reminded herself with a spurt of fear, was exactly what he was. The younger was tall and thin, with bony wrists protruding from the ends of his sleeves. His mid-brown hair was short and neat and, though both wore chain-store jackets and trousers, he'd taken trouble with shirt and tie.

Could something have gone wrong? she was wondering frantically. Had she made a mistake somewhere? But as they moved towards her, ludicrously out of place in such feminine surroundings, her professional smile was securely in place. If they'd come to arrest her, she wouldn't assist them by displaying apprehension.

'Good afternoon, gentlemen. May I help you?'

To Steve Cummings, the woman who had stood un-moving while they waded over the thick carpet seemed equally formidable. On the wrong side of seventy, she was ramrod straight in black linen tunic and tailored skirt. Her silver hair, though severely styled, was in keeping with her years, but her face was a mask, heavily rouged and eyeshadowed as though she were about to appear on some brightly lit stage. Heaven help them if this was Miss Tovey.

Beside him, the skipper cleared his throat. 'We'd like a word with Miss Tovey, please.'

Steve, watching the painted face, caught a fleeting expression of relief. What had the old bird been up to? he wondered with amusement. Exceeding the speed limit? Drunk in charge?

'I'm not sure if she's free. If you'd just wait a moment?'

She turned away to lift the phone on the satinwood desk behind her. From a screened area to their left came the tinkle of crockery and a smell of toasted teacakes. Nice little place they had here. Pricey though, he'd bet. Wiser not to mention it to Rita.

The gorgon turned back to them with a smile. 'That'll be all right, gentlemen. If you'll please follow me?'

She led the way up the curved staircase and across more carpeted expanses, where brocade sofas were positioned at intervals between rails of dresses and discreetly curtained alcoves lined the walls. Stopping at a door, she knocked, opened it, and ushered them in.

The woman who rose from the desk seemed altogether more approachable, with pretty, fair-to-grey hair and an attractive smile. 'Good afternoon. You wish to see me?'

'Detective-Sergeant Dawson, ma'am, and DC Cummings. You reported an abandoned vehicle, I believe?'

Her brow cleared. 'I did, yes. Have you traced the owner?'

'We have, but there are one or two questions we'd like to clear up.'

She gestured at a couple of chairs. 'Sit down. Would you like some tea?'

'That's very kind. Thank you.'

She spoke into an internal phone and Dawson cleared his throat. 'I know you've been through this before, ma'am, but I'd be glad if you'd bear with me. Could you tell us exactly how the van came to your notice?'

'Certainly. I'd just turned out my light on Monday night when I heard a car in difficulties. Then it ground to a halt and the driver tried several times to restart it. Since it sounded very close, I got out of bed to have a look.'

'And what exactly did you see? This could be important.'

'The van was directly under the street light, with the driver standing on the pavement looking helplessly up and down the road.'

'Can you describe him?'

She looked surprised. 'I thought he'd been contacted?' When Dawson kept silent, she shrugged and replied, 'He was of medium height, wearing a denim jacket and trousers.'

There was an interruption as a girl came in with a tray. No teacakes, Steve saw regretfully, but there were some interesting biscuits on a plate. These were passed round while Miss Tovey poured the tea and the girl handed them each a cup. Then she left the room.

'Anything else you noticed, ma'am?' Dawson prompted.

'Yes, he had red hair. I could see it quite clearly in the lamplight.'

'Age?'

'Twenties, I'd say. I only had a quick look, because as soon as he saw me I drew back.'

'*He saw you?*' Dawson leant forward urgently and his tea slopped in the saucer.

'Goodness, Sergeant, you made me jump! Yes, he saw me. Does it matter?'

'It might matter very much indeed.'

'But I don't understand. I thought—'

'Excuse me a minute. Are you absolutely certain that the man you saw was the driver of the vehicle?'

She stared at him in bewilderment. 'I don't understand,' she said again.

'You didn't actually see him get in or out of the van?'

'No. But it was the middle of the night, for heaven's sake, and there was no one else around.'

'Nevertheless, for the sake of argument, it is remotely possible that the driver had already left the vehicle and this man just happened to be standing beside it?'

'I don't for a moment think—'

'But it's *possible*?'

'If you say so.'

'You didn't see him lift the bonnet, or do anything to suggest he'd any connection with the van?'

'Other than stand beside it in an otherwise deserted street, no.'

Dawson drew a deep breath. 'Right. This man, whoever he was, saw you looking at him. How did he react?'

'I really don't know. As I told you, I let the curtain fall. But a minute later I heard him walking off down the hill. I thought he'd gone in search of petrol.'

'Did he seem worried when he saw you? Nervous at all?'

'I don't think so. He just looked up, our eyes met, and for a moment we stared at each other. Then I moved back. Look, let's stop playing games, shall we? What's all this about?'

'The man you saw, ma'am, might or might not have driven the van, but he certainly wasn't the owner.'

'How do you know?'

'Because,' Dawson said heavily, 'the owner and his twin brother were lying dead in the back of it.'

Monica put down her cup. 'Oh no! How absolutely awful!'

'So it seems likely,' Dawson continued, 'that if the man you saw *was* the driver, he was also the murderer. And he knows that you saw him.'

There was a short silence. Then Monica said levelly, 'So now what happens?'

'For a start, we'll arrange protection. And it would help if you could move to a friend's house for a while, till things die down.'

'But if he thought I was some kind of threat, wouldn't he have come after me already?'

'He might just be waiting for the opportunity.'

She thought for a moment. 'I see now why you were trying to cast doubt on his being the driver, but it won't wash, you know. It was a still night, and my window was open. I heard the car approach and stall. I heard him try to restart it. Later, I heard him walk away. If there'd been anyone else I'd have heard his footsteps too, and voices, because obviously they'd have spoken. So we really can't clutch at that straw.'

'Pity.'

'Yes, indeed. And protection's pretty pointless, too. He has only to look up the electoral register to track me down, and I lead a pretty high-profile life, as you doubtless know. Moving to someone else's house wouldn't help; I'd still have to appear in Court and come here every day. Just a minute.' Her voice sharpened. 'You say the driver *and his twin* were in the back?'

'Yes, ma'am. The White brothers, of Trafalgar Street.'

'Oh *dear*! It suddenly occurred to me it might be.'

'You know them?'

'They've been up before me several times, usually for soccer violence. I'd hoped we'd reform them in time.'

'It'll be in the records, but can you recall when they were last in Court?'

'Not offhand. Earlier this year, I think.'

'Doubtless there were other lads up with them, that they'd been fighting with?'

'Yes, half a dozen or more.'

'The same ones every time, or did they vary?'

'The Steeple Bayliss fans were always the same.'

Dawson grunted. Rivalry between the two towns dated back to Shillingham's superseding SB as the county town at the end of the last century.

Monica said frowningly, 'You think they could be responsible?'

'At this stage, ma'am, anyone could.'

'But the season's finished, hasn't it?'

'A week ago, yes. As it happens, the last match was an away one at Steeple Bayliss.'

'But surely any animosity of that type would be immediate? They'd hardly wait a week and then come over.'

'Unless something more serious had occurred, and it developed into a full-blown vendetta. The age of the man you described puts him in the right bracket.'

'In which case he won't be hanging round here, he'll have gone back to Steeple Bayliss.' Which was twenty-seven miles away, a good forty-five minutes' drive.

'All the same, it'll do no harm to be careful. I expect the DCI will put a policewoman in your house.'

'I hardly think that's necessary. In an emergency I can do as much as a policewoman. What I would appreciate, though, is someone keeping an eye on the house. If anyone tried to break in, it would be very upsetting for my mother.'

'I'm sure that can be arranged. Now, ma'am, if you'd be good enough to read through the statement DC Cummings has written out, perhaps you could sign it.'

Minutes later the policemen were shown out. Monica sat staring at the closed door, her normal, orderly life suddenly upside down. As a magistrate, she had long accepted that she could be the target of someone's spite—resentment over a sentence or even a misconstrued comment in Court. But the thought that she might be able to identify a murderer, and that he knew it, was distinctly unsettling. If only, she thought uselessly, she'd settled down earlier that night, not bothered to get out of bed, slept through the whole thing.

With a sigh she reached for the latest pile of catalogues.

CHAPTER 4

The post-mortem was held first thing the next morning. It was a part of his job that Webb had never become resigned to, and at this early hour he was finding it particularly trying. Broodingly he surveyed the circle of faces round the table: Steve Cummings, already green about the gills, Bob Dawson, Dick Hodges, Penrose, Smithers, each of them held in sickly fascination by the grisly task in hand.

Since even the Trubshaws had been unable to say with certainty which twin was which, Webb had resorted to fingerprints—fortunately on record—to establish that it was Gary White who had been stabbed.

During the last hour his clothing had been removed and examined closely, item by item, before being bagged for despatch to the laboratory. As expected, the tear in the green sweatshirt corresponded to the angle of the chest wound. Now, the high-powered lamps above the slab spotlit the naked young body as, ignoring the constantly flashing camera, Stapleton recorded his progress into the suspended microphone.

Slowly and with painstaking thoroughness the examination proceeded, the heat from the lamps and the pungent smell of disinfectant adding to the malaise of the onlookers.

They learned that the partially digested food appeared to have been in the stomach about four hours, which suggested death had occurred around 11.0 p.m. It had been caused by a single thrust of a short, serrated blade. No surprise there. The exact dimensions of the blade and the lethal path it had followed, Webb allowed to pass over his head. Such details would be on his desk in due course.

The hands of the clock circumnavigated its face and had started round it a second time before the body was removed and an identical one laid in its place: identical in all respects but one—there was no stab wound. In fact there were no external marks whatever on this second boy, a fact unusual enough in the circumstances to arouse curiosity. The performance started once more: intrusive incisions into the firm flesh, the removal and weighing of organs, the steady, expressionless voice speaking into the microphone.

Another hour and a half had passed before Stapleton announced it as his opinion that the deceased had died from vagal inhibition.

Webb stared at him in disbelief, his normal tact overwhelmed by frustration. 'You mean he stopped breathing? Oh, come on, doctor! That's how we all die!'

Stapleton fixed him with a cold eye over the top of his mask and continued as if he hadn't spoken. 'The malfunction appears to have been caused by trauma.'

'What kind of trauma?'

The pathologist raised thin shoulders. 'Shock? Fear?'

'You're saying he was frightened to death?' This time Webb strove to keep his voice neutral. But really! A healthy young thug, not averse to the odd punch-up and having led anything but a sheltered life, to have died from *fright*, like a dippy old spinster who finds a man in her bedroom?

'There is no defect in any of the organs, nor, as I expect to have confirmed when the specimens are analysed, is poison indicated. Digestion had progressed to the same degree as that of the first body, leading to the assumption that they died within minutes of each other.' He paused and cleared his throat raspingly. 'Sometimes, I understand, an abnormal affinity exists between twins; if he saw his brother killed, it's possible the trauma he suffered could have resulted in his own death.'

No one spoke for a minute. Then Stapleton pushed the microphone aside. 'So there you have it, Chief Inspector. That's the best I can do for you.'

Webb nodded his thanks and pushed his way through the swing doors into the blessedly cool tiled corridor. It was a brief respite, for outside the hot sun awaited him, glinting on the pathologist's sleekly polished car and burnishing the gravel to diamond-like brilliance. But it was a natural life-giving warmth, unlike the harsh white lights inside which illuminated death.

He paused, savouring his return to the living world, and drew a restorative breath. To his left lay the hospital grounds, spreading lawns, colourful borders and clusters of trees now in full leaf. On the terrace at the back of the building, dressing-gowned patients relaxed in the sunshine and in the distance a uniformed nurse was encouraging two others along one of the paths.

On Webb's right was the high wall which separated the hospital from Carrington Street Police Station. With a start he remembered the scheduled press conference and hastily checked his watch. He'd just about make it. Balance restored, he walked briskly down the drive and turned into the next gateway.

'Monica?'

'Hello, Justin.' She nodded at her secretary, and the girl picked up the pile of signed letters and quietly left the room. 'I thought you were away for a few days.'

'I am, but I just rang home and Eloise told me the news.'

'A bit shattering, isn't it?'

'Exchanging glances with a murderer? You could call it that. And what's this about refusing to move out of the house? You really must be guided by the police.'

'But, Justin, if he wants to track me down, hiding in

someone else's house won't stop him. I still have to go to
Court and run this place; I refuse to have my whole life
disrupted.'

'Better than losing it, I'd have thought.'

She suppressed a shiver. '*Touché*; but I'm not really being
foolhardy; the police are watching both the house and the
store, and they follow me everywhere. I'm as safe as I can
be in the circumstances.'

'How good a look did you get at him?'

'Fairly good; he was directly under the lamp.'

'You hadn't seen him before? In Court, for instance?'

'Not that I remember. Why?'

'I wondered if dumping the bodies on your doorstep was
deliberate.'

'No, I'm sure not. The engine was stuttering before it
reached the house and he tried to restart it. The fact that I
knew the twins was pure chance.'

'I hope you're right; it's quite bad enough as it is. Look,
why don't you move in with us for a few days?'

'No, really. It's sweet of you, but I'm all right. Anyway,
they'll probably nab him before long. There can't be that
many criminal redheads on the loose.'

'Ever heard of hair dye?' he asked drily.

But, as he'd anticipated, he'd been unable to change her
mind. Monica's adherence to her own ideas—her stubborn-
ness, in fact—was a quality he'd had to accept, since it was
one he shared. They'd clashed more than once over the
years, but their underlying affection for each other was
undiminished.

As he replaced the phone he was aware that the call had
done nothing to still his unease. Had he been her husband
rather than her brother-in-law, he might have stood more
chance of influencing her—though he doubted it. An inde-
pendent lady, Monica. George would have his hands full,
if and when they married.

He walked across the hotel bedroom and stared out of
the window at the busy street below. Monica's sudden
vulnerability had brought home to him how fond he was of

her, and for the first time in years he thought back to a time when they'd been even closer.

They'd met when he was just down from university and she studying to go into her father's business. Against the façade of the building opposite he conjured up a picture of her as she was then, a small, attractive girl with fair curls and laughing eyes. Yet even at that tender age she'd known where she was going, and he'd recognized a strength of purpose which matched his own. There was an immediate empathy between them; he'd taken her to the theatre and for long, candlelit dinners, over which they confided their ambitions for the future. Looking back, he realized that he'd been on the verge of falling in love with her. But, calling at her home one evening, he'd met Eloise—beautiful, spoilt Eloise, who at that time was engaged to Harry Marlow.

And that had been that. In the all-consuming selfishness of passion, both Harry and Monica were forgotten, and within weeks the wedding had taken place. Now, after all those years, Justin found himself belatedly wondering how Monica had felt. Of course, it wasn't as though there'd been any commitment between them, a fact which, if he'd thought about it at all, had eased the odd twinge of conscience. It failed to do so now. He could only hope she'd not been hurt as badly as Harry must have been. It said a lot for both Monica and Harry that they were still among their closest friends.

Gazing unseeingly out of the window, Justin continued to probe his suddenly sensitive conscience. For, having discarded Monica without a thought, he hadn't hesitated to call on her whenever it suited him. It was to her that he propounded his ideas for expansion, his worries about share prices or personality clashes among the staff. She was always ready to listen, calming unnecessary anxiety, offering sound comment and occasionally suggesting a course of action which he was glad to follow.

And over the last year or two his demands on her had extended into the social sphere as well. Eloise had never hidden her boredom with the fat Italians and balding

Frenchmen who came to do business with him and whose languages she made no attempt to understand. So, when she started to plead increasingly unconvincing migraines, he had turned to Monica, who had willingly placed at his disposal not only her fluency in languages but the quiet, attentive charm that was so much a part of her. In fact, he realized to his dismay that there were times when he preferred his sister-in-law's company to that of his wife.

A knock on the door made him start and he turned sharply.

'Justin?' a voice called. 'Coming down for a drink before lunch?'

'Be right with you!' he answered, and, thankfully relinquishing his musings, he went to join his colleagues.

The press conference over, Webb and Jackson had repaired to the Brown Bear for lunch, where they were joined by DI Crombie.

'Any developments while I was at the PM?' Webb asked him, as Crombie put down his plate and glass and pulled out a chair.

'The piece in last night's *News* produced some phone calls.' The local paper had run a front page item, asking if anyone had seen the van between 9.0 p.m. and midnight on Monday.

'Well?' Webb prompted, as the Inspector spread a paper napkin over his knees before embarking on his meal.

'Some lads walking home from the Mulberry Bush are pretty sure they saw the van parked along the road about ten forty-five. At any rate the one they saw was dirty, dark green in colour and had an elongated roof-rack. And at eleven-twenty or so a motorist pulled into the Wood Green lay-by to check a map reference and noticed a dark van parked there without lights. He didn't investigate—thought it was a courting couple.'

'So if both sightings were the van we're interested in, it had only moved a hundred yards in half an hour?'

'It would seem so.'

'Waiting for someone?'

Crombie shrugged.

'Did the lads see anyone in it?'

'Yes, they glanced in as they passed and a man was sitting behind the wheel. It was only a brief glimpse and they can't describe him, or say if there was anyone with him.'

'Well, it's not likely the murderer would have been hanging about with a couple of bodies in the back. So, always provided it was the right van, it seems the twins parked near the Mulberry Bush for a while, and later drove on to the lay-by. Any bright ideas why?'

'A call of nature?' Jackson suggested. Webb shot him a repressive glance.

'And there was another report,' Crombie continued. 'Not the van this time, but a parked car just round the bend from the lay-by. The bloke who rang in thought at the time it looked suspicious, because it was off the road hidden under some branches. As far as he could tell there was no one inside.'

'What time was this?'

'Also around eleven.'

'So the two vehicles were parked near each other?'

'No, Davis checked that when he took the call. The car was on the Shillingham side of the lay-by and the van on the far side, near the Mulberry Bush.'

'Close enough, though, not to rule out a connection between them. So where had the car driver got to, and why did he try to conceal his car? Do we know what make it was?'

'Not much of it was visible, but it looked like a hatchback.'

'Mm. Any other news?'

'The house-to-house didn't turn up much. All the neighbours noticed the van, but Miss Tovey was the only one who did anything about it. The rest of them ignored it, presumably in the hope that it would go away.'

Webb grunted. 'I take it all the people who phoned are coming in to make statements?'

'Yes, this afternoon, after which I'll drive out with them

to check the exact positions of the parked vehicles. In the meantime, though it's rather late now, the lay-by's been sealed off till the SOCOs can get to it.'

'Everything all right, gentlemen?' The barmaid bent forward to collect their empty plates, the bracelets on her wrists jangling discordantly. An inveterate sensation-seeker, she took great pride in her police clientele and constantly questioned them on current cases, seemingly undeterred by their unfailing refusal to be drawn.

'Fine, thanks, Mabel.'

'Working on the murder of them twins, are you?'

Webb winked at Crombie. 'That's right,' he admitted.

'Shocking thing, young lads like that. Mind, they weren't what you'd call squeaky-clean theirselves, were they?'

'Weren't they?'

'Come on, Mr Webb, you're not fooling me. All that hooligan business up at the club. Some say it's just high spirits, but I don't go along with that. It's violence, same as any other, and once you get into that sort of thing, there's no saying where it will end.'

'Very true, Mabel.'

She waited hopefully, but when it was apparent he was adding nothing further, she reluctantly moved to the next table.

Webb drained his glass. 'Speaking of which, has Bob been along to the club?'

Crombie grinned. 'You bet—any excuse! He hadn't got back by the time I left.'

'I wonder if he'll come up with anything new.'

As decreed by the Football Association, Shillingham United Supporters' Club had no official link with the football club. Nor had it any official premises, being based at a small commercial hotel, the Duckworth, a little further up Station Road. There, its members had the use of what was grandly known as the conference suite, which comprised a bar, a large room where social events were held and a small ante-room for committee meetings.

Bob Dawson, an ardent football fan, knew it well, but this was the first time he'd been there in an official capacity. He hoped young Steve's presence would reinforce his authority over what was normally a relaxed social gathering.

As it was lunch-time, several members who worked locally were gathered in the bar, talking in low voices. The news of the double murder had jolted them out of their flat, end-of-season feeling, and when they turned towards him, Dawson saw that his apprehension had been groundless. Whatever his usual relationship with them, they recognized him now as an officer of the law and were looking to him for reassurance.

Dick Turner, the chairman, came towards him with his hand extended. 'Glad to see you, er—Sergeant. A terrible business.'

'Yes, sir.' Dawson gratefully kept up the formality. 'This is my colleague, DC Cummings. Mr Turner, club chairman.'

Steve also had his hand shaken.

Dick Turner cleared his throat. 'We were just wondering if this is going to reflect on the club in any way? We've had our share of bad publicity, but nothing as serious as this, thank God.'

'Too early to say yet, sir. I'd be interested, though, to hear of anyone you might know of who's clashed with the Whites in the past.'

'But, good God, man, you know how they were!' Turner broke off, remembering Dawson's official hat, and continued more calmly. 'This is difficult, with the lads dead, but it has to be said they've caused us quite a few headaches over the years. They were loyal members of the club—none more so —but if there was any trouble at or around the ground, they were sure to be in the thick of it.'

Dawson nodded. 'They had their special cronies, didn't they?'

Turner shrugged. 'As to that, I couldn't say. Bill here knows more about the daily goings-on than I do.'

The club secretary came forward, his normally cheerful

face subdued. He nodded awkwardly to Dawson, embarrassed by his change of status.

'They were more hangers-on than cronies,' he said. 'It was an odd set-up—the twins were totally self-sufficient. There was something about them that set them apart, and it fascinated the other lads.' He drank from the tankard he was holding. 'They were known as the Lily-White Boys, you know; partly from their name and partly because they always dressed in green, the United colour.'

Dawson glanced at Steve, writing industriously in his notebook. Bill Johnson knew Dawson was aware of all this, and it was to Steve's notebook that he addressed his remarks.

'Anyway, the gang, such as it was, used to go drinking before matches. One season we tried closing the bar here until after the game, but it caused aggro with the other members and didn't stop the tearaways, who found another drinking hole.'

'If we could have the names, sir?' Dawson reminded him. He knew them, of course, but was interested to hear if Johnson's list tallied with his own.

'Jango Simms, Mike Leyton and Charlie Richards were the main ones. Sometimes Pete Seymour and Brian Arkwright joined them, but they were more on the fringe. Still, what's your interest in them? They were pals, not enemies.'

'They'd know any likely enemies, though.' Only a half-true answer, but it satisfied Johnson.

'Yes, of course. I see.'

'The last match of the season was at Steeple Bayliss, wasn't it?'

'That's right, the week before last. We beat them four–nil.'

'The White boys were there?'

'Yes. They didn't start any trouble, though; like the rest of us, they were over the moon at the result.'

'And they went straight home afterwards?'

The secretary frowned. 'I couldn't say. We'd laid on a coach, but they weren't on it—used their own transport.

Come to think of it, their van was still in the car park when we left.'

'Which was at what time?'

'About six.'

'What about their pals?'

'They were with us. I remember thinking the Whites must have told them to push off. They did that sometimes, when they wanted to be by themselves. As I said, it was a weird set-up.'

'So it's at least possible they could have got up to something after the rest of you had left.' Something which had serious repercussions a week later.

'I suppose so, yes.' Bill Johnson looked anxious, as though as secretary he was responsible for the conduct of his members.

'Right, we'll get on to the other lads and see if the Whites mentioned what they were planning to do. Thanks for your help, gentlemen. If there's anything else, we'll be in touch again.'

Not, Dawson thought, as Steve Cummings followed him out of the side door from the conference suite, that he himself had learned anything new. The point was what the Governor would be able to do with it.

It was five o'clock when Dick Hodges, the Chief SOCO, phoned.

'Thought you'd like to know we've finished going over the victims' room.'

'Anything of interest?'

'Not with regard to their deaths, as far as I can tell. No fingerprints other than their own and Mrs Trubshaw's. But there's a stash of what looks like stolen property, which might be helpful.'

Webb reached for pen and paper. 'Give me a quick run-through, will you, Dick?'

'Well, there's a handful of jewellery all bundled together. Nothing of enormous value, but some rather nice pieces— jade, coral, stuff like that. Plus a silver cigarette box inscribed LMB, some silver and ivory fish-eaters, a little jade statue and a couple of strings of pearls. I haven't checked if they're real or not—my guess is cultured—but I bet my old lady wouldn't turn her nose up at them.'

Webb grinned, thinking of Dick's 'old lady', a bright, vivacious forty-year-old. 'OK, thanks; I'll have them checked with the property index.'

'I've some news for you, Alan,' he told Crombie when, ten minutes later, the Inspector returned to his desk. 'Remember that house that was done on the SB to Marlton road? The one you thought might have some connection with the plane?'

'Yes?'

'It was the White twins who turned it over. Dick's found some of the stuff in their room.'

'What the hell were they doing out there?'

'At a guess, returning from SB after the match.' He'd just finished Dawson's report. 'From what I remember, the owners admitted leaving the garage doors open. The lads must have noticed as they drove past and stopped on spec.'

He shot a sly glance at the Inspector. 'I don't think the plane was theirs, though,' he added with mock seriousness, 'or we wouldn't have found anything in their room.' And he dodged, grinning, as Crombie flicked a paper dart in his direction.

CHAPTER 5

When Monica arrived home that evening, Mrs Bedale was in the hall replacing the telephone.

'Oh, Miss Tovey, there you are. That was a call for you.'

Monica paused, alerted by the woman's tone of voice. 'Yes?'

'I'm sorry, he wouldn't give me his name.'

'Did he leave a message?'

'Only that he'd ring back.'

Monica frowned. 'He asked for me specifically?'

'No, he said, "the lady". I asked which one, and he said "The one who works at the shop".'

'What did he sound like?'

Mrs Bedale twisted her apron. 'Not like a gentleman, madam.'

'I see. Thank you.' Monica walked past her and up the stairs, trying to ignore her quickened heartbeats. For there had been an unidentified call at the store, too, for which she'd also been unavailable. Her line had been engaged, the man was asked to hold on, and when the switchboard girl went back to him, he'd rung off. According to Patsy, that called had sounded 'a rough type'. The van driver? It seemed the most likely explanation.

In the privacy of her room, Monica tipped the contents of her handbag on to the bed and with fingers that shook a little picked up the card which the policeman had given her the previous day. It listed a number to ring should she need it, and a name other than his own—Detective Chief Inspector Webb. Sitting down on the bed, she pulled the extension phone towards her.

The Chief Inspector heard her out in silence. Then he asked, 'Will you be in for the rest of the evening, ma'am, if he does ring back?'

'No, I'm going out to dinner with friends.'

'At a restaurant?'

'No, a private house. Beechcroft Mansions.'

At the other end of the line Webb swallowed his surprise at hearing his own address. At least he could keep an eye on her.

'With your permission I'll have a listening device fitted to your phone. It'll only take a moment, and with luck we should trace the call. But we also need to know what he wants, and it seems he'll only speak to you. Is there a number you could leave with your housekeeper this evening?'

'Yes; Miss James is an old friend—I'm sure she wouldn't mind.'

So it was Hannah; he'd thought as much. 'In the mean-time, try not to feel nervous. As you know, you're being accompanied wherever you go, and should you need assistance it'll be immediately available.'

If that was intended to reassure her, Monica thought, replacing the phone, it had had the opposite effect. Was he expecting someone to jump out at her? She shuddered and went to run her bath, leaving the connecting door open so she could hear the phone. It didn't ring.

The four of them had been at Ashbourne School together, though not as exact contemporaries: Monica and Gwen Rutherford were already prefects when Hannah and Dilys joined the school. Now, Gwen was headmistress and Hannah her deputy, while Dilys had found her niche with a series of highly acclaimed novels. The two separate friendships, formed in schooldays, had, over the years, amalgamated to encompass four successful, unmarried women who enjoyed each other's company and who tried to meet once a month to visit the theatre or a concert or to dine at each other's houses.

Gwen and Dilys were already there when Hannah showed Monica into the sitting-room. The local press had stated where the van was found, and although Monica's name was not mentioned, her friends didn't doubt she was the 'local resident' who'd reported it to the police.

She fended off their sympathetic queries with a smile. 'No, I didn't look inside, thank God. By the way, Hannah, I hope you don't mind, but I've left your phone number with Mrs Bedale. There've been two unexplained calls today, both of which I've missed. Chief Inspector Webb thinks I should take the next one.'

'Of course—no problem,' Hannah replied, adding casually, 'He knows you're coming here—Mr Webb?'

'Yes, but he'd have found out anyway, since I have watchdogs on my tail who follow me everywhere.'

Gwen frowned. 'I don't understand. The fact that the van happened to be left outside your door surely doesn't put you in any danger?'

'Unfortunately I saw it being left.' That, at least, hadn't been in the paper.

'But he—the murderer—couldn't know that?' Dilys this time.

'Again unfortunately, yes, he does. Because he looked up and saw me watching him.'

There was a short silence. Then Hannah said jerkily, 'No wonder you have police protection. Why didn't you tell me? You could have come and stayed here till it blew over.'

'That's sweet of you, and Justin and Eloise said the same, but it wouldn't have done any good. He must have looked me up in the electoral register, because he rang the store too. Short of holing myself up somewhere and remaining completely incommunicado, there's really nothing I can do.'

'In your place that's exactly what I'd have done,' said Dilys with a shiver.

Monica smiled. 'Fortunately my imagination isn't as fertile as yours.'

Hannah said determinedly, 'Well, if the phone does go, at least we're all here to back you up. So let's forget about it and enjoy our evening. Gwen, your glass is empty: more sherry?'

The evening passed. The conversation was as bright and interesting as usual, but for Monica at least the underlying strain could not be forgotten. Occasionally her eyes strayed to the squat shape of the phone on the polished table. It remained uncompromisingly silent. Had he rung home again, and panicked when given another number, suspecting a trap? Should she have cancelled this engagement and stayed in to speak to him? Most certainly she should not! she answered herself indignantly. As she'd told Justin, she refused to have her life disrupted by this stranger. And what had he replied? *Better than losing it, I'd have thought.*

'Monica?'

She looked up guiltily to meet Hannah's concerned eyes. 'I'm sorry—did you say something?'

'I wondered if you'd like more coffee?'

'No, thank you. In fact, I think I should be going. I mustn't keep my watchdogs from their kennels.' She looked round the table at their carefully unconcerned faces. 'I've been like Banquo's ghost this evening, haven't I? Sorry if I've spoiled things.'

They protested loyally, but Monica suspected they were relieved when she left them. Getting into her car at the gate, she was aware of the other vehicle parked a few yards back and grateful for the reassuring flick of its lights. She did not, however, realize that from a darkened window on the top floor of the building she'd just left, DCI Webb himself watched her set off for home.

For a while she was able to keep the police car in view in her mirror, but on reaching the town centre she lost it in the traffic. No doubt it was behind there somewhere. She circumvented Gloucester Circus and turned into the High Street, its pavements still busy on this warm evening but with a crowd different from the harassed shoppers who populated it by day. The night people, she thought fancifully. Then she had left it behind, and as the buildings grew more sparse the gap between the street lamps lengthened and she drove for several minutes through open land before the houses began again and she turned off for North Park.

A few headlights were visible in her rearview mirror. One set no doubt belonged to her bodyguard. Along North Park Drive the lamps glowed brightly, and the hall light shone in her own doorway. She drove past it and turned down the side road leading to the garages, aware for the first time of the contrast between the brightly lit road at the front and the deepness of the shadows which edged the mews.

Reaching the garage she drew to a halt, its doors illuminated in the beam of her headlamps. Where the hell were those policemen? Well, she wasn't going to sit here waiting for them. Slamming out of the car, she walked into the circle of brilliance. A spotlit target, whispered a little voice inside her. Ignoring it, she bent to pull up the garage door, and as she did so a sudden rustle behind her spun her round in time to see a dark figure move back into the shadows. Fear sluiced over her in a scalding tide. Without thought she flattened herself against the door, feeling the wood still warm from the day's sunshine under her splayed fingers. 'Who are you?' she cried hoarsely. 'What do you want?'

After what seemed an eternity the figure moved forward again and as she opened her mouth to scream, a voice said, 'Police, ma'am. Sorry if we scared you.'

'*Scared* me?' She hardly recognized her voice. 'You're supposed to be looking after me, not giving me a heart attack.'

Dry-mouthed and humiliated by her fear, she turned back to the door, releasing the catch so that it swung upwards. She got into the car, drove it carefully inside and relocked the garage. Ignoring the muttered 'Good night' from the shadows, she wrestled with the lock of the garden door until it opened to admit her and, slipping inside, slammed and locked it behind her.

As always, the lights of the house welcomed her at the far end of the garden. Normally she loved entering from the dark mews and walking towards the light; it was part of coming home at the end of the day, anticipating the warmth and companionship within. Tonight, she was conscious only of the shrubbery edging the path, the large patches of shadow against the wall. It took all her self-discipline not to break into a run, and it was with overwhelming relief that she gained the sanctuary of the house and went up the steps to the hall door.

It was past eleven and her mother'd gone to bed. With held breath Monica advanced to the telephone table. There were no messages awaiting her. He had not phoned back. *Damn* him! she thought in an explosion of relief. Damn him for ruining her evening, and that of her friends. Until those terrifying moments in the mews, she hadn't realized just how fearful the mysterious phone calls and the Chief Inspector's bland reassurance had left her.

Her breathing was still uneven and she paused to steady it, letting her eyes move lovingly over the graceful hallway. Its handsome proportions and restful atmosphere had frequently restored her over the years when despair or frustration had laid her low. That it was more than just a passageway was confirmed by the way visitors tended to linger in it, admiring the prints on its ivory walls, the colourful Persian rug, the antique tables.

She was suddenly very tired. Reaction, no doubt, to the stresses of the day. Switching off the lights, she went slowly up the stairs, leaning heavily on the banister like an old woman. It was at times like this, she thought ruefully, that it would be good to be married; to have someone in whom to confide your fear, someone to reassure and protect you. Briefly she thought of her brother-in-law. A pity he was in Worcester. And from him her mind went, as it usually did, to George. Perhaps one day he would take first rather than second place in her thoughts, but until then—

On an impulse she lifted the phone and dialled his number. It rang several times, and she wondered belatedly if he were in bed. At least his mother wouldn't be disturbed; her bedside phone was switched off when she settled for the night.

Monica was about to replace the receiver when a breathless voice said, 'Yes? Latimer speaking.'

'George, it's me. I hope I haven't woken you?'

'Monica! Is everything all right?'

'Yes, of course. I'm sorry, I shouldn't have disturbed you. But I've just got in, Mother's in bed, and I—I needed to talk to someone.'

'I wanted to speak to you, too. In fact, I did phone earlier but was told it was your girls' night out.'

'You rang here? There was no message.'

'I told Mrs B. not to bother. I was only going to offer my sympathy over that beastly van. You mentioned it at the Teals', I remember. What an appalling experience for you.'

Perhaps, then, the other man had also phoned, but as before left no message? Her heart started pounding again.

'Monica? Something *is* wrong.'

She said wearily, 'I shouldn't worry you with all this, particularly at this time of night.'

'It's what I'm here for. You know that. What's happened?'

'There was one thing I didn't mention at the dinner-party, because I didn't think it important. When the van broke down outside the house, I got out of bed to have a look. The driver was out on the pavement by that time. And he looked up and saw me watching him.'

'My God!' George said softly.

'What's more, there've been a couple of phone calls today which I've not been able to take.'

'Anonymous calls, you mean?'

'I suppose they were, in a way. At any rate, he wouldn't leave his name. And according to Mrs Bedale, he "didn't sound like a gentleman".'

'You think it's the murderer?'

'I don't know who else it could be.'

'But—'

'George, it's all right, really. I have police protection— they follow me wherever I go. No one can get at me.' Please God.

'Does Justin know about this?'

She closed her eyes briefly. 'That the man saw me, yes. He's away on business and Eloise told him over the phone. But not about the calls.'

'He should have insisted you moved to his house straight away. I wish to God I could have you here, but Mother would promptly die, just to be difficult.'

In spite of the strain, she gave a little laugh. 'I wish you were here,' she said impulsively, surprising herself by meaning it.

'My darling girl.'

'But as you're not,' she continued with deliberate lightness, 'I shall go to my narrow bed alone.'

'Shall I arrange one of our weekends? It's a long time since we got away.'

The eagerness in his voice touched her. 'That would be lovely, but let's get this business behind us first.' She paused, then added with unusual humility, 'Thank you for being so patient with me, George.' And before he could call her his darling girl again, she hung up.

When the last of her guests had gone, Hannah went up the flight of stairs to Webb's flat. It was several days since she'd seen him, which, in their unconventional relationship, was not unusual. The demands they made on each other varied according to need, from casual friendship to passionate lovemaking. Totally relaxed with each other and content with the tacitly imposed 'no strings' embargo, they were aware how fortunate they were.

He opened the door while her finger was still on the bell. 'I thought you'd come up when they left.'

'I suppose you were holding a watching brief from your eyrie,' she commented, going past him into the flat. 'Monica was escorted home, I take it?'

'Most definitely. I watched the procession set off myself.'

Hannah walked to the window and stood looking down the hill towards the lights of Shillingham.

'Is she in danger, David?'

'It's difficult to say. The man must realize she's had ample opportunity to pass on his description. Short of fingering him in an ID parade, there's little else she can do.'

'She's pretty jumpy. Unusual for Monica, she's normally such a cool customer.'

'She said you were old friends?'

'Dating back to school, though she's older than I am. I only got to know her well a few years ago, through Gwen, who was her contemporary.'

'Who else was at your dinner-party?' he asked, handing her a glass of brandy.

'Gwen, and Dilys Hayward.'

'Ah yes, you've mentioned her before. Didn't they do one of her sagas on TV a couple of years back?'

'That's right, *Changing Times*. It's being made into a film now.'

'You make a formidable group, the four of you.'

She smiled, but absently, looking into her glass. 'Do you know anything about the boys who were killed?'

'They were football hooligans, for a start.'

She looked up. 'You think that's why they died?'

'Could be. Rivalry with another team—probably SB. I've asked Chris Ledbetter to rope in his lot and interview them.' DI Ledbetter ran a tight ship at Steeple Bayliss and knew all the local trouble-makers.

'But you don't really think that was the motive, do you?'

'Well, they were involved in other shady dealings—breaking and entering, shoplifting. Continually up before the magistrates—including Miss Tovey—but we could never make it stick. To hear them plead, you'd think they were pure as the driven snow. Lily-White Boys indeed.'

'Gang warfare, then, between small-time crooks?'

'A possibility if they'd been found in some back alley. But in North Park Drive?'

'Ah, but that was a mistake, wasn't it? The van broke down.'

'True. But what was it doing there in the first place? We've had reports of it being seen out by the Mulberry Bush on the Chipping Claydon road and again in the Wood Green lay-by. From there, there's a direct road back to Shillingham without looping round North Park.'

'You don't think it was deliberately left at Monica's house?' Hannah's eyes were troubled.

'It seems to have been a genuine breakdown. According to Miss Tovey, he tried several times to restart it, but it was out of petrol. All the same, it's the devil of a coincidence that she knew the twins.'

He looked at her grave face and the tawny hair that fell forward as she stared frowningly into her glass. Gently he removed it from her hand. 'Still, it's nearly midnight, and no time to be thinking of vans and bodies and football hooligans. I've something much more interesting in mind.'

She smiled and moved into his arms. 'Really?'

He laid his cheek against her hair. 'Have you turned off the lights downstairs?'

'Yes.'

'And put the leftovers in the fridge so the cat can't get at them?'

She smiled into his shoulder. 'Yes.'

'Really, Miss James, anyone might be forgiven for thinking you came up here to seduce me!'

And he effectively cut off any reply she might have made.

Across the town, Harry and Claudia Marlow were lying side by side in the big canopied bed. When she heard her husband sigh and turn over for the third time in as many minutes, Claudia reached up and switched on the light.

'Can't you sleep?'

'No, I keep going over the arrangements for the Private View.' He owned a small but prestigious art gallery in Carlton Road.

'No problems, are there?'

'Not as long as someone turns up. We've had hardly any replies so far.'

'Everyone leaves it to the last minute.'

'That's all very well, but how many do we cater for? We're laying on canapés and wine, you know.'

'Just order the same as last time. I've mentioned it to several people—I'm sure there'll be a respectable number.'

He gave a short laugh. 'I'm even wondering if Mrs Jones posted the invitations—she's missed things before. With working only part-time, it seems as if only half her mind's on the job.'

'Get rid of her, then,' Claudia said.

'Oh, she's all right really. I'm just being paranoid.'

They lay in silence for a while, busy with their own thoughts. He'd not asked what was keeping her awake, but if he had, she could not have told him. Ever since Abbie's casual remark, she'd tormented herself with the thought that he might still be attracted to Eloise. To her shame, she'd even set little traps for him, hidden, innocent-seeming pitfalls that, whether intentionally or not, he'd adroitly managed to dodge.

Still watching him as he lay staring at the ceiling, she consciously stripped away the intimacy of twenty-odd years, looking at him as she would a stranger. And what she saw disconcerted her: a man no longer young, tense—how long had that pulse beat at his temple?—disillusioned, perhaps, since there were shadows on his face that familiarity had hidden from her. His hair was greyer than she'd realized, and his jawline slacker. She said softly, 'Oh, Harry!'

'Um?' He turned to her, and her focus shifted, returning him to her as the man she had married.

'You look worn out,' she said.

'Well, things have been fairly hectic, as you know. The price of success, my love.'

'Then perhaps the price is too high. Is it getting too much for you? You spend more and more time at the Gallery—' Or was he in fact seeing Eloise? She hurried on: 'Why not leave it to Tony for a few months and we can take a long cruise or something. It would do us both good to get away.' Away from Eloise.

'Claudia, for God's sake! I mention we haven't had many replies for the Private View, and the next thing you have me throwing up the Gallery and careering off on a world cruise! What's got into you?'

'You looked so tired, darling. I suddenly panicked.'

'Well, there's no need to. That Gallery's my baby and I'm not handing it over to anyone. Anyway, there's no hassle; Tony looks after the everyday running of the place. I just have the fun part, buying, borrowing, showing.' And the financial responsibility, she thought.

She turned off the light and leant over to kiss him. 'All right, Mr Tycoon, just as long as you can switch off when you come home and let your wife get some sleep!'

'I'll do my best.'

She turned on her side, tucking the duvet under her chin. As she was dropping off to sleep, she murmured drowsily, 'But we can go on a cruise sometime, can't we?'

There was no reply.

CHAPTER 6

Webb said reflectively, 'The Whites were window-cleaners, you know.'

Crombie didn't look up. 'So?'

'I was just wondering if they might have seen something they shouldn't have.'

'"While cleanin' winders?"' Crombie asked with a grin.

'Could be. We'll have to see all their customers. Come to that, they could have found something incriminating at the house they burgled.'

'And tried blackmail?'

'It's well within their province. Pike tried to phone the owners last night about the recovery of their goods, but there was no reply. Rather than ring back, Jackson and I'll go along and see if we come up with anything.'

It was a lovely day for a drive, and Webb felt his spirits lift as they drove out of town. If only he had his paintbox with him to record the summer countryside: waist-high cow parsley under hedges festooned with hawthorn; heavy-laden chestnuts, their green canopies studded with waxy candles; rounded hills spiked with steeples and fields brilliant with rapeseed. In such surroundings it was hard to believe that murder had brought them here.

The Heronry, some miles outside Marlton, was an isolated house standing just above the road. Its intricate gates, closed now, had been left open on the night of the robbery, as had the doors of the garage, which Webb noted were clearly visible from the road.

Jackson went to open the gates and they drove up the immaculately gravelled driveway. In the centre of the lawn to their left a stone heron stood sentinel over an ornamental pond. Very plush, Jackson conceded, though he preferred a less formal approach himself. As he drew up in front of the house, the door opened and a woman came hurrying down the steps. She stopped short on seeing them and frowned, watching as the two men climbed out of the car.

'Is it important?' she demanded. 'I've an appointment at the hairdresser's in twenty minutes.'

'We believe it's important, yes, ma'am. Chief Inspector Webb, Shillingham CID.'

'Oh.' She hesitated, glanced pointedly at her watch. 'Well, all right. You'd better come in.'

The hall was wide and bright, sunlight flooding down the staircase from a window half way up it. A woman appeared from a rear door and their hostess said, 'It's all right, Molly, these gentlemen want a word with me.'

She led them into a room full of beautiful, highly polished furniture, where every surface was covered with Dresden, Meissen, crystal and silver. You'd think with this lot they'd have more than a tuppeny-ha'penny alarm system, Jackson marvelled. All in all, he considered the Whites had been very abstemious.

'Now, what is it? Have you caught the men who broke in?'

'In a manner of speaking. They're both dead.'

'Dead?' she repeated, her voice rising.

'Not as a result of the burglary,' Webb assured her, his mouth twitching at her apparent mental picture of a shoot-out to recover her belongings. He went on to give her a brief outline of what had happened, while Jackson looked her over with a jaundiced eye. Aged around fifty, she was one of those lean, tanned women with muscular arms and legs and a discontented expression. She was wearing a silk dress splashed with poppies and high-heeled sandals, and her toenails were the same vermilion as her fingernails.

'I know you spoke to the local police, Mrs Badderley,' Webb was saying, 'but I'd be grateful if you could tell me again just what was taken.'

'Do I really have to go through that now?' she exclaimed pettishly. 'If I don't leave soon, I'll miss my appointment.'

Webb's eyes moved dispassionately over the frizzy head.

'We won't keep you any longer than necessary. The list, Mrs Badderley.'

She gave an exasperated sigh and recited rapidly, like a child with its twice-times tables, 'Silver cigarette-box, case of fish-eaters, jade statue, jade necklace, two coral brooches, two strands of pearls.'

'That was all?' Webb asked in surprise as she came to a halt. In that case, the twins hadn't shifted anything and they'd recovered the lot.

'All? Isn't it enough?'

He looked expressively at the laden tables and mantel-shelf, and she flushed a little. 'Well, yes, I suppose we were lucky they didn't take more. But it's not only the things missing, Chief Inspector. It's the feeling that strangers have been poking about among one's personal possessions.'

Webb glanced at the antique bureau against the wall. 'Is that desk locked?'

'No, why?'

'You're sure nothing was taken from there?'

She lifted her eyebrows. 'There's nothing in it worth taking.'

'What exactly is in it, Mrs Badderley?'

'Share certificates, passports—' She broke off and, rising, walked quickly to the desk and lowered the front, rifling through the pigeonholes. Then she turned back. 'You had me worried for a moment, but everything seems to be in order.'

'You're not missing any personal papers, letters or anything.'

'No. But why should burglars be interested in that kind of thing?'

'Blackmail, perhaps?'

Oh-oh! Jackson thought, as Mrs Badderley drew herself up, an ugly colour flooding face and neck. 'Would you please explain that remark? It sounds very much as though you're suggesting we've done something to be ashamed of.'

Webb spread his hands. 'Most people have secrets of some sort. It needn't be anything very—'

'I think you'd better go, Chief Inspector. In any case, I really can't spare you any more time at the moment. If you want to discuss this further, I suggest you return when my husband is here.'

She was obviously used to dealing with recalcitrant tradesmen, Webb thought. Signalling to Jackson, he too rose to his feet. As she gestured him imperiously towards the door, he said slowly, 'There was one other reason for our coming; to let you know we've recovered everything that was taken.'

'Oh.' Looking slightly discomfited, she added, 'Good, I'm very glad to hear it. When may we claim them?'

'You can call in at Carrington Street Police Station at your convenience. Good day, Mrs Badderley. I hope you're in time for your hair appointment.'

'Old bat!' Jackson commented, starting up the engine as Mrs Badderley hurried down the steps and round to the garage.

'It's a wonder they realized anything was missing,' Webb said. 'A real Aladdin's cave in there.'

'I'm surprised the lads didn't help themselves to more.'

'Well, a lot of that stuff is easily identifiable. I'd guess their fence is pretty cagey about what he handles. Nothing heavy—just easily portable knick-knacks that fetch a good price and no questions asked.'

'Lucky for us they hadn't got shot of it.'

'Yes, but according to their landlady they've left stuff lying around before. My guess is their fence isn't local.'

'Do you reckon Mrs High-and-Mighty *was* being black-mailed?'

'I'd like to see anybody try!' Webb said.

The White twins had belonged to a section of society that was not at home with a pen. Though required to keep basic records of their work for tax purposes, these were minimal indeed, nor were any notes of a more personal nature found in their room. It seemed to Crombie that whatever they'd seen, or learned, or guessed, which had caused their deaths had gone with them to the grave—as doubtless their murderer had intended.

At least such records as there were, were all in one place, since they had no business premises. An odd paper or two might have been stuffed in the dashboard of the van, but they'd have to wait till the SOCOs had finished with it to check.

The phone sounded on his desk and as he lifted it, there was the sound of money dropping into a machine. A timid female voice said in his ear, 'Could I speak to the gentleman in charge of the White murders, please?'

Crombie straightened, looking at Webb's empty desk. 'He isn't here at the moment, but I'm working on the case. Can I help you?'

'Well . . .' Obviously she was doubtful of his qualifications.

'I'm Detective-Inspector Crombie,' he added, hoping his full rank would impress her. It did.

'I suppose that's all right, then. Only—' Her voice shook. 'I'm their aunt, you see.'

'Indeed?' Crombie's surprise rang in his voice. 'We were under the impression they had no relatives.'

'I know, I saw it in the paper. That's why I'm ringing.'

'And your name is—?'

'Mrs Hargreaves.'

'And your address, Mrs Hargreaves?'

'Two, River Close, Oxbury.'

Oxbury; thirty-three miles due west of Shillingham. If he could catch Dave before he left the Marlton area, it would be quicker to go cross-country from there.

'Will you be home all day, ma'am?'

'I can arrange to be, yes.'

'Then either DCI Webb or I will be out to see you. Thank you very much for calling.'

Crombie replaced the phone and immediately lifted it again. An aunt; now there was a turn-up for the books.

*

The car-phone rang as they were re-entering Marlton and Jackson was looking out for a pub in which to have lunch. There was a nice-looking one on the opposite corner and he slowed down, waiting till the Governor had finished his call.

'Well, there's a thing, Ken!' Webb commented then. 'The Whites have some relatives after all: an uncle and aunt living in Oxbury. They just phoned in.'

'Took their time, didn't they? It was in the papers Wednesday evening.'

'We'll find out why when we see them. OK,' he added, as Jackson opened his mouth, 'we'll eat first, and that place over there will fit the bill nicely.'

'Fair clocking up the miles today, aren't we?' Jackson commented, driving round to the car park behind the pub.

'Just the day for seeing a bit of the countryside.'

They had their lunch in the little back garden under a gaily striped umbrella. Friday was market day, and the pub was quite busy.

'Old Trubshaw was very definite there were no relations,' Webb said through his ham sandwich. 'My guess is they didn't keep in touch with the twins, so I don't suppose they'll be much help. Still, anything we can find out about their background will be a bonus.'

Half an hour later they were on the road again, and still the sun shone. Webb loosened his tie and wound down the car window, resting his arm on the frame and gazing out at the rich fields and the trees with their summer foliage silvered by the wind. For the first time in years he allowed himself to think back to his childhood and the market garden his parents had owned. They'd expected him to go in with them when he left school, but instead he'd run away from home and joined the police. There were good enough reasons for his leaving, but he didn't want to dwell on them now. In any case, he had no regrets. He enjoyed his work, though he remained a countryman at heart.

The little market town of Oxbury lay just ahead of them, nestling in a curve of the river. Its main claim to fame was

Greystones College, one of two boys' public schools in the county.

'River Close, you said, Guv?' Jackson turned down towards the water. 'Remember walking along here with that young lad from the College?'

'Yep. The nursery rhymes case. Nasty one that.' He sighed, still entangled with memories. 'Come to that, they're all nasty.'

River Close was in fact set well above the water, which it overlooked. It consisted of a few thatched cottages, pretty enough in their vivid gardens, with pale-starred clematis frothing over walls and wisteria swathed round doorways. However, Jackson, being of a practical turn of mind, bet they still had privies at the back, and wouldn't have swapped one for his cosy little semi.

No. 2 had a slightly shabby look; the roof was in need of re-thatching and the paintwork round the windows was flaked and dirty. They walked up the path and rang the bell. The woman who opened the door looked pale and down-trodden. Her limp hair hung lifelessly round her face and she wore a faded print dress and scuffed sandals. Very different from the elegant Mrs Badderley at The Heronry.

'Mrs Hargreaves? Chief Inspector Webb and Sergeant Jackson, Shillingham CID.'

She nodded and stood aside and they walked into the small, dark hall and thence, at her direction, into the front room with its brick chimney-breast and diamond-paned windows.

'You'll wonder why I didn't phone earlier,' she began defensively, 'but Roddie said it was none of our business and I should let it go.' She surveyed them helplessly, twisting her hands together. 'But I couldn't. After all, they were my sister's boys and they'd lived with us for eight years.'

Webb raised his eyebrows. 'We were told they'd been brought up in an orphanage.'

She looked indignant. 'They never were! They came to us when they were seven; their parents were killed in a coach crash coming home from holiday. And it was never easy, Inspector, that I must say. We've a girl and boy of our own, and the twins were always ganging up on them. Every day there was an upset of some kind or other.'

Small wonder, Webb reflected, with two adults and four children in a cottage this size.

Since they'd still not been invited to sit, he took the initiative and lowered himself cautiously on to a cane-bottomed chair in need of repair. Jackson, after a moment's hesitation, perched gingerly on the edge of the sofa. Their hostess remained standing, eyeing them apprehensively.

'So they left about five years ago?'

'It must be going on for that. They were getting to be a real worry, staying out all night and bringing boys we didn't like to the house.'

'They'd have still been at school then?'

'And that was another thing,' she said plaintively. 'The man from County Court was always on at us about them not showing up. How were we supposed to know? They left home at half-eight every morning and came back at four. Of course we thought they were at school.'

'Was leaving their idea, or did you turn them out?'

She looked uncomfortable. 'Half and half, you might say. Roddie's not a patient man, and they'd been getting him down for a while. Then one night they came home late and brought some of their gang with them. We were in bed, and they started playing records and shouting and laughing. So Roddie went down and found them smoking pot. Well, he went spare. Threw their mates out of the house, and ranted and raved at them, threatening all sorts. In the end I put on my dressing-gown and went to try and calm things down, but the drugs were the last straw. Roddie was frightened, see, that our own two might be tempted. I don't remember who first said about getting out, but the twins went next morning, taking their belongings with them.'

'They were only fifteen,' Webb said. 'Didn't you report them missing, or try to find out where they were?'

Avoiding his eyes, she shook her head. 'We didn't want them back, you see. Roddie said we were well shot of them.'

'You never heard anything more of them?'

'No.'

'So you can't give me any idea who they spent their time with? Any friends or enemies they might have made?'

'They didn't have friends, not the way our two did. They didn't need anyone but each other. As to enemies—' She shrugged. 'Who knows? Other football fans, I suppose. Even when they were little, they were football-mad.'

Webb said casually, 'What did you and your husband do on Monday evening, Mrs Hargreaves?'

'Monday? Same as always. I watched *Coronation Street* while I did the ironing and Roddie went to the pub.'

'What time did he get back?'

'Just after closing time.'

'Has he a car?'

She looked at him worriedly, aware that his interest had now switched to her husband but not knowing why. 'He never takes it when he goes drinking—doesn't want the police breathing down his neck.' She stopped, remembering who her visitors were. 'Anyway,' she added hastily, 'there's no need. The Stag's only up the lane.'

'He wasn't later home than usual last Monday?'

'No.' Her eyes widened as the penny finally dropped. 'You're never thinking Roddie had anything to do with it? The murder? He might have a quick temper, Inspector, but he'd never hurt the boys. After all, they were *family*.'

Nevertheless, Webb made a note to have Hargreaves interviewed. Suppose the twins *had* tried to re-establish contact, and he couldn't face the possibility of becoming embroiled with them again? Especially now his own children had reached an age more likely to be susceptible to drug-pushers. Suppose they'd been persistent, abusive even, and his acknowledged quick temper had got the better of him?

With his mind on a new set of permutations, Webb took his leave of Mrs Hargreaves and he and Jackson returned to Shillingham.

*

Abbie Marlow suddenly clutched at her friend's arm. 'Look!' she exclaimed, jerking her head across the road. 'There's Theo! I wonder where he's off to at this time of day.'

Since both their mothers were out, the girls had decided to skip revision for the afternoon. Their first exam was still ten days away and the sunshine beckoned, so they'd taken the bus down the hill into Shillingham.

Mandy obediently looked at the tall, rather long-haired figure walking purposefully along the opposite pavement. 'So that's the famous heart-throb,' she remarked noncommittally.

'Let's follow him!' Abbie said impulsively.

'Why on earth?'

'Well, we've nothing better to do. It'd be fun.'

'But he'll only be going back to the office after lunch.'

'No, he's walking in the wrong direction. Come on, Mandy, just for a few minutes.'

'I suppose you're hoping he'll see you and invite you to that garden-party thing,' Mandy said resignedly.

But she allowed herself to be pulled across the road and they started after their prey, who by this time was some hundred yards ahead. He was walking quickly, his long legs carrying him effortlessly over the ground so that the girls had to break into an occasional run to keep him in sight. Half way down Duke Street he turned into a side road that led to the public park.

'Seems we're not the only ones playing truant,' Mandy said breathlessly as they took the corner after him. 'Perhaps he's going to feed the ducks!'

In fact, her facetious comment seemed uncannily accurate; having entered the park, Theo did indeed make his way towards the duckpond, the two girls still in cautious pursuit. But then events took an unexpected turn: a girl who had been sitting on one of the benches jumped up and ran towards him, sliding her arms round his neck as they embraced. Abbie stiffened, and Mandy patted her arm consolingly.

But Theo had already broken free and was talking urgently, watching his companion's face as he did so and occasionally looking quickly about him as though to check that they were unobserved. Each time, the watchers ducked down just in time to avoid detection.

Having responded eagerly to him at first, the girl now seemed to be holding back, lifting her hands expressively as she tried to make some point, until finally he caught hold of her and gave her a none too gentle shake. With a shrug of resignation she turned back to the bench where she'd left a carrier bag and, feeling inside, took out a large envelope. He almost snatched it out of her hands.

'What on earth—?' Abbie said under her breath. She exchanged a puzzled look with Mandy, and when they turned back to the pair, Theo was walking quickly away in the opposite direction, leaving the girl standing by the bench. As the two younger girls watched in even more bewilderment, she sank back on to it and covered her face with her hands.

Quietly, wishing somehow that they hadn't seen the encounter, they crept away.

Every time the phone rang that day Monica's mouth went dry, but it was never the mysterious caller. If, yesterday, he'd needed to speak to her so urgently, why was it no longer necessary? She found herself unable to concentrate, her mind continually returning to the puzzle.

One of the callers, around lunch-time, was George.

'Nothing further to report,' Monica told him wryly.

'Well, don't worry about it. It couldn't have been important, or he'd have rung back.'

'All the same, it's annoying not knowing who he was.'

'How about coming to the theatre this evening, to take your mind off things?'

'That sounds very tempting.'

'And supper afterwards?'

'I'd like to, George. Thank you.'

'Does your shadow have to come as well?'

'Only at a discreet distance. You wouldn't notice if you didn't know.'

'As long as I don't have to pay for her ticket!'

Monica was smiling as she replaced the phone. She knew her late-night phone call was responsible for this invitation, and it made her realize how luke-warm had been her response to him over the last few months. Poor George, he deserved better.

The phone rang again and again she jumped. But the switchboard girl was announcing the Duchess of Hampshire's secretary. Lord, yes, the wedding outfit. She'd forgotten all about it, which showed how preoccupied she'd been. Switching off her personal problems, she thankfully turned to the comforting familiarity of her work.

'An aunt?' Sid Trubshaw was staring at them almost belligerently. 'I don't believe it!'

'We've no reason to doubt the relationship,' Webb said mildly.

'But they told us they was orphans. Brought up in an orphanage.'

'Which one, Mr Trubshaw?'

'Well, I don't know, do I? Since they're Broadshire lads, I assumed it was the Derrisbrick.'

Webb nodded, seeing in his mind's eye the large, forbidding building on the outskirts of Ashmartin. A happy enough place inside, though, as he'd heard more than once. 'We checked,' he said. 'With the Derrisbrick and all the other orphanages in the country. None of them had any record of the White twins.'

'Another of their fairy tales,' put in Mrs Trubshaw tartly.

'But they wouldn't have *lied*,' her husband protested with defiant loyalty. 'Not to us. Mind, if the aunt and uncle threw them out when they was only nippers, they don't deserve to be called family. P'raps that's what they meant.'

Tactfully diverting the conversation, Webb continued, 'You told us they'd been with you about three years. Where were they immediately before, do you know?' 'Two years were still unaccounted for after leaving the Hargreaves.

'Yes, in digs on the Bridgefield estate.' Trubshaw shot a glance at his tight-lipped wife. 'Doris here insisted on references before she'd accept them.'

'Mind, to read it you'd have thought we were getting a couple of saints,' she said with a sniff.

Anyone who'd housed the White twins, Webb reflected, would be too eager to be rid of them to be scrupulous about references. 'Have you their address?' he asked.

'No, but I remember the name. Preston.'

'What reason did the twins give for leaving there?'

'Wanted to be nearer the town, for their job.' Trubshaw smiled sadly. 'And nearer the club, and all.'

Their job; inquiries in that direction had not been enlightening.

'What areas did they cover with their window-cleaning?'

'The centre of town. Commercial premises, like. No private houses.'

Which was interesting. 'Station Road?' All kinds of nefarious practices went on there; plenty of scope for possible blackmail.

'Aye, but the smart part too. Carlton Road, East Parade, Duke Street.'

'Thank you, Mr Trubshaw,' Webb said slowly, 'you've both been very helpful.'

'Have they?' Jackson asked in surprise, on the way back down the path.

'Oh yes. Quite apart from the Prestons, who are well worth a visit, we now have some idea of their round. It's an interesting thought, Ken, that Miss Tovey herself might have been a customer. Her shop's in East Parade, isn't it?' He got into the car. 'And I'm still not convinced they were left at her house by chance. See, what I always come up against is why the murderer didn't leave well alone. OK, he bundled them into the van so they wouldn't be seen. But why didn't he then hot-foot it back to his own car and get the hell out of it? Why climb into his victims' van and start careering all over North Park, with the evidence of his crime jogging around in the back? It only makes sense if he'd some idea of getting even with someone. Suppose he'd a grudge against Miss Tovey, and wanted to give her a fright?'

'It still wouldn't be worth taking that risk, surely? As far as we know he wasn't used to the van; for all he knew, it could have had faulty lights or brakes or something, and one of our blokes might have stopped him. And what about the fact that it really did run out of petrol outside her house? He couldn't have gauged that so exactly, could he? Anyway, if it was someone who knew her well enough to have a grudge, she'd have recognized him, wouldn't she?'

Webb sighed. 'You're right, Ken, none of it fits. All the same, it'd be interesting to find out how many of Miss Tovey's acquaintances had their windows cleaned by the Lily-white Boys.'

CHAPTER 7

Back at his office, a note awaited Webb asking him to phone Dick Hodges. Perhaps things were moving at last.

'Ah, Dave. Thought you'd like to know we came across traces of blood in the Wood Green lay-by and we've established it's definitely that of the stab-victim. So at least we've found the scene.'

'Well done, Dick. Anything where the vehicles were parked?'

'Spots of oil on the main road where the van was, which match up OK, and broken branches and flattened grass on the other side of the lay-by. Something was parked under the trees all right. What's more, a track had been made through the shrubbery to the back of the lay-by.'

Webb gave a low whistle. 'That's pretty conclusive, I'd say.'

'It should be, once you have a suspect. He left fibres and the odd shoe-print behind him.'

'Well, that's encouraging. Thanks, Dick.' Webb replaced

the phone and ran his hand over his face. What they now had to discover was where the twins had been between 9.0 p.m. when they left their lodgings and 11.0, when they were seen near the Mulberry Bush, a drive of only about twenty minutes. Why had they parked there? Were they waiting for someone, or indulging in a bit of spying? The other party involved was almost certainly the driver of the possible hatchback under the trees. But perhaps it was he who was spying on them? If they were meeting by arrangement, why hadn't he driven openly into the lay-by, as the twins later did, instead of creeping round through the undergrowth? Because the murder was premeditated?

There was a tap on the door and Dawson poked his head round. 'Spare us a couple of minutes, Guv?'

'Of course, Bob. Come in and pull up a chair.'

Dawson did so, subsiding on to it with a groan of relief and stretching out his legs. 'Been pounding round the town on the track of the White gang. Now the season's over it's not so easy to run them to earth, specially since they've been avoiding the Duckworth.'

'Probably dodging all the speculation.'

'Yep—understandable. Anyway, I caught up with two of them at the timber yard where they work. Richards and Seymour. Couple of right layabouts.'

'Were they any help?'

'None whatever. Same story we hear everywhere—the twins kept themselves to themselves. If they were indulging in a spot of blackmail, they seem to have kept their mouths shut about it.'

'Were any members of the gang closer to the Whites than the rest of them?'

'Possibly Jango Simms. He was what Seymour called their "leg man", whatever that means.'

'Let's hope it means confidant. We've had a bit of luck today; the twins have an uncle and aunt alive and well and living in Oxbury. In fact, they lived there themselves until five years ago.'

'Get away! Not what they told their landlord, was it?'

'No, poor old bugger. It hit him pretty hard.'

'What of the relatives?'

'They took the twins in when they were orphaned at the age of seven and kept them, under increasing difficulty, for eight years.'

'Reckon they deserve a medal!' Dawson observed, with a sour grin. 'Then what happened?'

'An almighty row about noise, unacceptable friends and pot-smoking.'

'And they got out?'

'Yep. Never to be heard of again. Or so the aunt says.'

'You don't believe her?'

'I don't know. She seems frightened of her husband; he didn't want her to contact us. I keep wondering why. Like a job for tomorrow?'

'Surprise me!'

'It'll give you a break from the football crowd, at any rate. Leave Cummings to track down—what were their names?—Arkwright and Leyton, and you can attend to Simms yourself after you've seen Hargreaves. I haven't got his work address, but he should be home on a Saturday. Two, Riverside Close. But don't rile him, Bob; we don't want to get his wife into trouble.'

'You know me, Guv,' Dawson said laconically. 'The soul of discretion.'

Miss Tulip closed the gate of the little Victorian house carefully behind her, counted, as she always did, the number of footsteps it took to reach the front door—unfailingly nine —and inserted her key. But this evening the familiar ritual failed to soothe her. The police had been back at the store asking questions, and she was deeply disturbed.

Closing and locking the front door behind her, she went at once to the parlour cupboard, took out her father's sherry decanter and poured herself a generous measure. But instead of sitting down to enjoy it, she remained standing, an immobile figure in black jacket and skirt, gazing unseeingly through the net curtains to the matching terrace across the road.

Why were the police still nosing around? She didn't for a moment think it was anything to do with Miss Monica. Not directly, that is. After all, anyone could see it wasn't her fault that a couple of bodies had been left at her door. Miss Tulip shuddered delicately and took another gulp of sherry.

Then there was the phone call Patsy had spoken about; an uncouth sort of fellow, wanting to speak to Miss Monica. That, again, had filled her with fear. Suppose whoever-he-was had discovered her little secret and wanted to report her? Would Miss Monica give her notice? Without Randall Tovey's to go to every day, her life would have no meaning, no meaning at all. Beside that possibility, even her—her secret was unimportant.

Setting down the sherry glass with a decisive little click, Miss Tulip went back into the lobby and dialled a number. When the familiar voice answered, she identified herself and asked crisply, 'Has anyone been making inquiries about me?'

'Not a soul, me love.' She heard the surprise in his voice, and it was some comfort.

'I'm uneasy, Mr Spratt. I shan't be contacting you for a week or two, and—this is *most* important—you must make no attempt whatever to contact me.'

'You're the boss.' He sounded supremely unconcerned, quite incurious as to her anxiety.

'Very well. I'll speak to you in due course.'

She breathed a sigh of relief as she replaced the phone on its cradle. Then, some minutes behind her normal schedule, she went upstairs, slightly unsteady after the unaccustomed sherry. In the neat, impersonal bedroom she changed out of her working clothes and hung them carefully in the wardrobe till the next morning. She now had roughly fourteen hours before she could return to her real home, the foyer of Randall Tovey. She would fill them, as she usually did, with music, tapestry and sleep. As far as the police were concerned, she'd taken such precautions as she could. Now she must sit back and trust there'd be no further developments.

With a small sigh, she went downstairs to prepare her frugal supper.

Monica heard the car as she finished dressing for the theatre and went to the window expecting to see George. Instead, it was Justin who was coming up the path. The bell rang as she gathered up handbag and stole, and she reached the bottom of the stairs as Mrs Bedale admitted him. He stopped short on seeing her.

'You're going out?'

'In a minute or two, yes.' She held up her face for his usual peck. 'To what do we owe this honour?' He seldom called at the house without Eloise.

'I wanted to satisfy myself that you're all right.'

'Oh, Justin,' she said softly. 'That's very sweet of you.' It occurred to her that he'd driven straight here on his return from his business trip. 'I'm fine,' she added.

'No further developments?'

'Look, come in for a drink. Mother will be pleased to see you.'

'Don't change the subject, Monica. Has something else happened?'

'A couple of phone calls, that's all.'

His voice sharpened. 'What kind of phone calls?'

'A man wanted to speak to me, but I wasn't available either time.' She laid a hand on his arm. 'The police know about it. It's all right.'

'It's very definitely *not* all right,' he said vehemently. 'I'd be much happier if you packed an overnight case and came back with me now. And your mother too, if she'd like to.'

'Really, it's not necessary. In any case, he hasn't phoned today, so whatever it was couldn't have been important.'

He was about to argue further when the doorbell sounded again. He turned and opened the door to see George on the step.

'Am I interrupting something?' George inquired, looking from one of them to the other.

'Justin's just heard about the phone calls.'

'There haven't been any more?'

'No, nothing. As I say, that's probably the end of it.'

Justin said heavily, 'I mustn't detain you. Are you going
somewhere interesting?'

'To the Grand, to see the new Ayckbourn play. I thought
we could both do with a laugh.'

'Is that George, dear?' called a voice from the drawing-
room.

Justin said quickly, 'I really mustn't stop—I've not been
home yet.'

George said, 'Don't worry, we'll cover for you' and he
opened the drawing-room door. 'Good evening, Maude.
How are you today?' As he went into the room he pulled
the door to behind him, allowing Justin to make his escape
undetected.

In the hall, Monica said steadily, 'George will take care
of me.'

'I'm sure he will. Why the devil don't you marry him,
and tell his mother to go to hell? Then perhaps I could stop
worrying about you.'

The outburst was so uncharacteristic that Monica stared
at him, and after a moment he managed a sheepish smile.

'Sorry, it's been a long day.'

'I know, and it was sweet of you to make this detour on
the way home.'

He wished she wouldn't keep calling him 'sweet', but he
daren't cause any more ripples.

'Just as long as you're all right.' He put up his hand and
briefly touched her cheek. Then he turned and let himself
out of the house, closing the door silently behind him. It
was several seconds before Monica walked slowly to the
drawing-room door.

'You're later than I expected,' Eloise remarked, as her
husband bent to kiss her.

'I looked in at North Park to check that all was well.'

Eloise lifted an eyebrow. 'And was it?'

'Yes; Monica's going to the theatre with George. She should be safe enough with him.'

'Safe? Good heavens, Justin, you don't seriously think she's in danger?'

Her light, almost mocking tone irritated him. He was tired, he reminded himself, crossing to the drinks cabinet. 'Yes, as it happens, I do. She's had a couple of anonymous phone calls, you know.'

'I didn't know, but it's an acknowledged fact that the people who make them are harmless. They get rid of their aggression or whatever that way.'

'I wasn't aware you were a psychologist, Eloise.'

'My, my! We are grumpy this evening!'

'Darling, I'm sorry.' Contritely he went back and kissed her again. 'I've had an exhausting three days and frankly I could do without this worry now.'

'Then let George handle it. You said he could cope. Look, I know it was ghastly for Monica to have that beastly van there and actually to see the man, but it's in the hands of the police now, and they seem to be watching over her.'

'Yes, I know.' He drew a deep breath. He'd forgotten about the bodyguard.

'I wish she'd marry George,' Eloise continued, accepting the refilled glass her husband handed her. 'Goodness knows, they're ideally suited.'

Justin, aware she was echoing his own sentiments of half an hour before, nevertheless looked at her in surprise. 'You really think so?'

'Of course; Monica needs someone to boss about, and George needs to be bossed. After a lifetime with Ethel, he'd be lost with no one to tell him what to do.'

'Don't make the mistake of underestimating George,' Justin warned her. 'He's very well thought of in the business world.'

'Oh, I'm sure he's most worthy,' Eloise said carelessly. 'He just bores me rigid.'

'Who does, dearest Mama?' Theo had come into the room, unnoticed by his parents.

'George Latimer.'

'Oh, agreed. A real drag.'

'Theo, you're speaking of one of our friends,' Justin said sharply, wishing his son would act rather less like a Sloane Ranger.

'Mother started it!' Theo retorted, unrepentant. He wandered over to the drinks cabinet and poured himself a Campari. 'By the way, has your invitation to the Private View arrived?'

'Of course, ages ago.' Eloise sipped her drink.

'It's on Tuesday, isn't it? I haven't had one, but Claudia issued a general invitation when she was here. I'm sure it'll be all right if I turn up.'

'Even more all right if you buy a painting.'

'At those prices? You must be joking.'

'So why go?' asked his father. 'For the free drinks?'

Theo threw him a reproachful look. 'You meet interesting people at those do's, businesswise as well as socially. Come on, Dad, that's why you go yourself! Mother's the only arty member of the family.'

Eloise smiled complacently. She and the Marlows were members of the local Arts Appreciation Society, which involved attending monthly lectures, visiting museums, churches and Stately Homes, and going on three or four trips abroad each year. The family teased her about it, regarding it as one of her 'trivial pursuits' along with bridge and her passion for clothes, but she ignored them, merely pointing out that they all benefited from her eye for unusual trinkets and the objets d'art which decorated their home.

'Of course you should go, darling,' she told her son. 'I'm sure it was an oversight, not inviting you. Anyway, Claudia was saying there haven't been many replies; they'll be grateful to you for swelling the numbers.'

Justin, who had never in his life been anywhere uninvited, could only hope she was right.

By the next morning the weather had clouded over, and the river Kittle which flowed through Oxbury was correspondingly grey. Little gusts of wind whipped its water into ripples and ruffled the feathers of the waterfowl that swam there. Bob Dawson, having left his car at the top of the lane, hoped the rain would hold off until he got back to it.

Wild goose chase, this, in his opinion, and despite what the Governor had said, he'd have been better pursuing his inquiries at the club. They knew him there, and young Steve was out of his depth. Still, his not to reason why, and at least he had Simms to see this afternoon. If he could find him, that is. He turned into Riverside Close and went up the path of No. 2. An unshaven man in shirt-sleeves opened the door. 'Yes?' he said uninvitingly.

'Detective-Sergeant Dawson, sir, Shillingham CID. Could I have a word?'

Alarm flooded the ruddy face and its colour receded. 'Police? Must have the wrong address.'

'Mr Hargreaves?' He nodded mutely. 'I've a few questions concerning your nephews, sir, Gary and Robert White.'

The man put out a hand to support himself against the door-frame. Dawson, interested, wondered if he were going to pass out.

'How—?' Hargreaves swallowed and tried again. 'How did you know about that?'

'If I could just come inside for a minute, sir?'

Grudgingly the man stood aside. He exuded an earthy smell of stale sweat and tobacco.

'Who is it, Roddie?' A frail-looking woman appeared at the back of the hall, a bundle of washing in her arms. Her eyes widened at the sight of Dawson.

'It's the police, for Gawd's sake.' He turned to her, suddenly suspicious. 'Kathleen, you never—?'

'I saw two men yesterday,' she faltered. 'There was no harm in it, Roddie, and I felt we should. I—didn't think anyone else would come.'

'You stupid cow! What did you want to do that for? I *told* you—'

Dawson, mindful of his mission to protect Mrs

Hargreaves, cleared his throat. 'Your wife behaved quite correctly, sir. I'm just following up—'

Hargreaves flung his way into the front room. 'You'd better come in here and get it over with. I'll deal with her later.'

But Mrs Hargreaves had more spunk than Dawson had given her credit for. 'I'd like to come in too, if that's all right,' she said, and although her voice shook, there was no mistaking her determination.

'Quite all right by me, ma'am.' All to the good, in fact. She was more likely to let something slip than was the surly devil she was married to. Hargreaves himself glowered at her but made no comment, and Dawson realized, to his considerable relief, that despite the Governor's unease she was not afraid of her husband. It seemed she suffered nothing worse than occasional hard words, and knew how to deal with him.

'Now, Mr Hargreaves, could you tell me how you spent last Monday evening?'

The man darted a glance at him. There was a long pause, then he said, 'I went to the pub, didn't I?'

'Which pub, sir?'

Another silence. Mrs Hargreaves was now looking bewildered. 'Why don't you tell him, Roddie?' Then, as her husband still didn't speak, she added, 'It's the Stag, sir, at the top of the lane. I did tell the other gentlemen.'

Dawson was about to ask Hargreaves to confirm this seemingly innocent fact, when the man burst out suddenly, 'You know, don't you? You bloody know!'

Dawson tried to look suitably knowledgeable without having the slightest idea what he was talking about. 'Did you in fact go to the Stag public house, sir?' he began tentatively.

'Of course I did, at first. But it was the darts match, wasn't it?'

Mrs Hargreaves put a hand to her mouth. 'I'd forgotten that.'

The significance was lost on Dawson, but fortunately Hargreaves, having decided his cover was blown, was now continuing. 'We were playing away, see. A coach came for us at half-seven and ran us over to the Magpie at Chedbury.'

Dawson and Mrs Hargreaves waited expectantly, and he lifted his shoulders in a gesture of resignation. 'And they were there, weren't they?'

Dawson stared at him blankly, and it was the woman who whispered, 'The *twins*? You saw the twins *on Monday*?'

'Now do you see why I didn't want us involved? But oh no, you had to have your way and get in touch with the police.'

'But—what were they doing out there?'

'I didn't ask them.'

'Did they see you?'

'Oh, they saw me all right. Came over, bold as brass and watched me playing darts. Fair put me off my aim, I can tell you.' Hargreaves stared down at the threadbare carpet, reliving the encounter.

'What time did they arrive?' Dawson interrupted, trying to assess this unexpected development.

'Nine-thirty, ten.'

'Alone, or with anyone?'

'Just the two of them, as far as I could see.'

'How—how did they seem?' asked their aunt, with somewhat belated concern.

'Full of the joys. I was expecting them to make trouble, but far from it. Even bought me a drink. They never mentioned us throwing them out, just said they were settled in Shillingham with a nice old geezer and his wife.' Hargreaves frowned, remembering. 'But there was something —I dunno—*odd* about them. Like kids, hugging a secret no one else knows. It made me nervous. I was waiting for something to happen, like they used to play me up in the old days. But they were as pally as you please, asking after you and the kids and everything.'

'Then what happened?'

'Nothing, really. They watched the darts and played the

slot machines, and then the coach came to collect us so they said goodbye.'

'What time was this, Mr Hargreaves?'

'Around half-ten.'

'And they asked after me,' his wife repeated, with tears in her eyes. Her husband nodded, his eyes still on the carpet.

Dawson drew a breath. 'Mr Hargreaves, why didn't you tell your wife you'd seen her nephews?'

She gave a little start, as though the question hadn't occurred to her. 'Yes, Roddie, why didn't you?'

He sighed. 'I was turning it over all the way home, thinking first one way then the other. But there'd been enough upset when they left, and I—well, I reckoned you blamed me for them going. I didn't want it all raked up again. Then when I got in you were half asleep and seemed to have forgotten about the match. So I reckoned if you were thinking I'd been at the Stag all evening, that was fine by me.'

'It must have been a shock to read of their deaths,' Dawson prompted.

'Knocked me sideways. Hearing nothing from them all these years, then catching up with them right at the end. But I was glad I'd said nothing to Kathleen. They were part of the past, and even so she shed a few tears. If she'd known I'd seen them the night they died, it would have been that much worse.'

'You didn't think that by coming forward you could have helped police inquiries?' But Dawson knew the answer to that one. Though basically a decent man, Roddie Hargreaves came from a stock which did not volunteer help to the police.

There seemed little more he could add, but at least his unwilling testimony had filled in the missing two hours in the twins' schedule. It hadn't, after all, been a wasted visit.

'The Magpie at Chedbury,' Webb repeated thoughtfully. Dawson had joined him and Jackson at their usual table in the Brown Bear.

'At least he's in the clear himself, Guv. He went back to Oxbury on the coach with the others.'

'Mm. What I was thinking was that, cross-country, it's only about five miles from Chedbury to the Mulberry Bush. If the lads had an appointment in the lay-by for eleven, they were probably filling in time. Wouldn't want to show themselves in the vicinity, so they couldn't drink at the Bush; and if they'd been on their home patch it would have caused comment if they'd left early.' He drained his tankard. 'Well done, Bob, you've filled in that missing two hours we were worried about. Pity it doesn't give us any clue about what happened later.'

'They must have left the Magpie soon after the coach did,' Jackson put in, 'if they were seen near the Mulberry Bush at ten forty-five.'

Webb nodded. 'What intrigues me is how Hargreaves described them—"like kids hugging a secret". Over-excited, hardly able to contain themselves. Mrs Trubshaw noticed the same thing. Obviously they had great hopes of Monday evening.'

'Lolly?' queried Jackson succinctly.

'Quite probably. Blackmail lolly. But who were they hoping to collect from? When we know that, we'll know the murderer.'

But on that score, Jango Simms couldn't help them. Dawson finally tracked him down at his home in Conduit Street, where it seemed he'd been intending to spend the day in bed. With bad grace he descended the rickety stairs in a dirty T-shirt and jeans, his spiky hair still rumpled from sleep, whereupon his mother bundled both him and Dawson out of the back door into the 'garden' to get out from under her feet. The dreary plot of land thus designated grew only nettles, bindweed and the odd thistle, and such grass as there was had scorched in the warm dry weather. The noise of express trains from the nearby track punctuated their conversation, but all in all it was preferable to the fetid atmosphere inside the house.

Jango, a leggy youth with purple and orange hair and one earring, was droopy and despondent, partly because he was still half asleep and partly from the death of the twins, who had added a bit of glamour to his drab life.

'How long had you known the Whites?' Dawson asked, proffering a cigarette by way of enticement. Jango took one and absent-mindedly tucked it behind his ear.

'Five years, give or take.'

'Before they came to live here?'

'Yeah, they was out Bridgefield then. Met 'em at the club.'

'And you were in their gang?'

That earned him a swift glance from suddenly wide-awake eyes. 'Nothing wrong with that.'

'But you were hauled up before the beak more than once, weren't you?'

Jango shrugged, neither confirming nor denying. Dawson decided to appeal to his vanity.

'Pete Seymour and Charlie Richards said you were the closest to the twins.'

'Yeah. Well.' Jango kicked at an inoffensive thistle.

'In on their plans, were you?'

The boy hesitated, longing to claim importance but aware that any questioning could dispel it. 'They didn't confide in no one,' he said reluctantly. 'Half the time, we didn't even know what they was saying. Talked in a kind of shorthand. Gave you quite a turn at first, but it made them kind of special.'

Dawson tried to keep his voice casual. 'Did you see them on Monday evening?'

The boy shook his head.

'When was the last time?'

'Sunday dinner-time.'

'How did they seem?'

'Fine. I was right cheesed off, with the end of the season and all, but they was all bright-eyed and bushy-tailed. Every now and then they'd look at each other and burst out laughing, but they wouldn't tell us what the joke was. Can't believe they've gone,' he added suddenly. 'It don't seem possible, somehow.' He bit his lip and turned abruptly away.

At least the White twins had not died unmourned, Dawson thought. Old Trubshaw, Mrs Hargreaves, Jango here. All, in their own way, grieved for them, which was more than a lot of people could expect these days. With which sombre thought he patted the lad's arm and left him, letting himself out through the side gate in order to avoid the house and Mrs Simms.

CHAPTER 8

It was Sunday morning, and Monica, obeying an instinct she didn't analyse, had decided to attend eight o'clock service at the local church.

St Stephen's, North Park, was a large and handsome building, built at the end of the eighteenth century to minister to the needs of the wealthy families who were moving into the new houses round about. No doubt its originators had expected it to be generously supported in perpetuity. Nowadays, however, its normal congregation numbered about fifty, and to Monica's shame she was not among them. She was a twice-a-year Christian, she admitted wryly, attending at Christmas and Easter, and for the rest of the year expecting the church's amenities to be available as and when she needed them—for baptisms, marriages and funerals.

Quietly letting herself out of the house, she set off on foot up the hill, not even troubling to check if her bodyguard was up this early on a Sunday morning. Yesterday's cloud had persisted, but so far the rain held off. The gardens needed it, everyone said.

She reached the gate of the churchyard and walked up the long path between well-tended lawns and graceful old trees. Fortunately the cemetery was some distance away; she was in no mood to contemplate mortality.

The sidesman at the door, whom she knew in his weekday guise as the local dentist, tactfully hid his surprise at seeing her. 'Good morning, Miss Tovey,' he murmured in his Sunday voice, pressing a leather book into her hand. Monica experienced a momentary panic: suppose they were using the new service, and she wouldn't be able to follow it? But a hasty glance down revealed the 1662 Prayer Book, well known from schooldays.

She took a seat in one of the back pews and looked about her, at the vaulting arch overhead, and at the ornate pulpit and carved pew-ends inflicted on the building by over-zealous Victorians. No sunshine this morning to fire the stained-glass behind the altar, but the grey light was more in keeping with her mood. In the silence the sound of bird-song came through the open door, and the unique church aroma of polish, old leather and flowers filled her nostrils.

Why hadn't he phoned back?

The unbidden thought intruded on her peace, shattering it like a strident bell and setting her nerves jangling. Grimly she fought it down, willing herself to concentrate on her immediate surroundings, and gradually her breathing steadied. The blackbird still sang outside, and from behind her came the low growl of Colonel Plumpton, the church-warden, as he checked the day's readings. Impossible to imagine, in this haven of peace, that somewhere out there, beyond the quiet churchyard and its protecting yews, was someone who wished her harm.

Yet wasn't that why she'd come here, to bargain with the Almighty? Please take this danger from me, and I'll be a better person in future? No doubt a familiar plea in this place, but how many of those who'd prayed it over the last two hundred years had been face to face with a murderer?

There was a rustle as those not already kneeling slipped to their knees, and the Vicar and server came through from the vestry. The service began, and as Monica joined in the familiar words, the sense of peace she'd been seeking at last filtered over her. Whatever the outcome of the next few days, she was grateful for it.

'Mrs Bedale tells me you've been to church,' Maude greeted her daughter, as Monica came into her room for breakfast.

'That's right.'

'Why was that, dear? There's nothing special on, is there?'

'No, I just felt like going.'

It seemed no further explanation was forthcoming, so Maude let it pass. There were times when she didn't understand Monica.

'Eloise phoned a few minutes ago,' she said, tapping her egg. 'She's invited us for lunch.'

'Two invitations in a week? We are honoured.'

'I told her it was their turn to come here, but she seems to think we need to get out of the house.'

The wider implications of the past week had, by mutual consent, been kept from their mother, but Eloise was right: Monica had no wish to spend a third day waiting for the telephone. 'That's kind of her,' she said.

Harry came back into the kitchen. 'That was Eloise on the phone. Maude and Monica are going for lunch, and she's asked the three of us to join them.'

Claudia turned from the joint she was studding with garlic. 'I hope you said no?'

He looked uncomfortable. 'I thought it would save you bothering.'

'But I already have bothered! Harry, it's eleven o'clock! The vegetables are prepared, the dessert's made, and I'm just about to put this in the oven. Anyway, we were at their house on Tuesday. What's the point of seeing them again so soon?'

Harry eyed the joint. 'But since you *haven't* put it in the oven, we could have it tomorrow.'

'Maybe, but I'm telling you I don't want to go. I was looking forward to a lazy family day with the papers; why should we be dragged along to help Eloise entertain her family?'

'That's not a very nice thing to say.'

'I don't feel very nice. I just don't want all the bother of having to change and make-up and do something with my hair, just because Her Ladyship takes it into her head at this late hour to ask us to lunch. Anyway, she must have known I'd have it all in hand.'

'Why bother changing? You look perfectly all right as you are,' Harry said with male obtuseness.

Claudia regarded him with exasperation. 'You think I could hold my own with Eloise in a shirt and cords?'

'Hold your own?' he repeated, and there was an odd note in his voice.

She turned to face him, aware that without realizing it, they'd crossed some kind of barrier and were on dangerous ground. What had she said to Abbie, less than a week ago? *Eloise is my friend as much as Daddy's.* Had that ever been true, when she had always been conscious of the need to be on her mettle?

'You know what I mean. She's always so well groomed.'

'But it's only lunch, for heaven's sake, not a Buckingham Palace garden party!'

'That's not the point. Whatever the occasion, Eloise will be perfectly dressed for it.'

'And there's something wrong with that?'

Claudia sighed, giving up the attempt to explain. 'No, Harry, there's nothing wrong with it. But I do wish she'd sometimes get it wrong, like the rest of us.'

'I'd no idea you disliked her so much,' he said.

'I don't dislike her, for heaven's sake, I simply don't want to go for lunch!'

'Well, I'm sorry but we're committed now. If you feel strongly enough about it, you'll have to ring her back yourself.'

'What are we committed to?' Abbie had wandered into the kitchen.

'Lunch at the Teals',' Claudia said heavily.

Abbie brightened. 'Me too?'

'You too,' Harry confirmed, ruffling her hair. 'You don't think we'd leave you alone on a Sunday?'

'Abbie has revision to do,' Claudia said, and was appalled at the waspishness in her voice.

'Oh, Mum, I'm up to here with revision! I'll do some more this evening, but please let me come with you!'

Claudia met Harry's accusing gaze and knew she was beaten. 'All right,' she said.

Abbie gave a little skip of pleasure and Harry walked out of the room. Stupidly close to tears, Claudia tore a piece of aluminium foil off the roll, tucked it round the joint and replaced it in the fridge. Then, with a bad grace, she went upstairs to wash, change, and recurl her hair. Whatever Harry might say, it was of more importance than ever that she should meet Eloise Teal on equal terms.

The landlord at the Magpie was affronted. 'What are you fellers trying to do to me?' he demanded. 'This is the second time in six months you've come in here and told me one of my customers has got himself murdered! Straight after leaving here, what's more!'

Webb made a placatory gesture, remembering Ted Baxter who'd met his fate at the hands of the April Rainers.

'What do you think it's doing to my trade?' the man was continuing. He indicated the row of drinkers at the bar. 'Times are bad enough, with all this talk about drinking and driving. If they keep on murdering what customers I've got left, I'll soon be out of business!'

'At least these two weren't regulars,' put in his wife consolingly.

'That makes a difference? I'm trying to encourage new business, not kill off any passing trade that looks in.'

Webb said soothingly, 'I'm sorry, Mr Teasdale, I realize it's upsetting for you but I need to check a few facts. You say you'd never seen these young men before?'

'Never set eyes on 'em.'

'Did you notice if they spoke to anyone while they were here?'

'They were chatting to the darts teams.'

'Was there any argument or unpleasantness?'

'None at all. They had a couple of pints each, played the fruit machines and watched the darts. We could do with more customers like them.'

'Have you any idea what time they arrived?'

'I don't clock my customers in and out, mate. Monday evening, that's all I can tell you.'

'They left when the Stag coach went,' volunteered his wife. 'I thought it was because the man they'd been talking to had gone.'

'And that was at what time?'

'Just after ten-thirty, wasn't it, Bert?'

'Round about, I suppose.'

'They didn't leave with anyone else?'

'As to that, I couldn't say. Quite a few were moving off around that time.'

It was remotely possible, Webb supposed, that they could have been killed completely on spec by someone who followed them from the Magpie. He didn't believe it, though. The feverish excitement, the parked van along the Chipping Claydon road, the hatchback under the trees: to his mind, all these spoke of a prearranged meeting, and the only contact the Whites had had at the Magpie was with Roddie Hargreaves, who'd gone back to Oxbury on the coach.

He had another half to soothe Teasdale's ruffled feathers, then Jackson drove him back to DHQ.

Though still overcast, the day had become warmer and more humid, making every action an effort, and pressure behind Monica's eyes warned her that a migraine was imminent. As she changed to go out to lunch, she acknowledged to herself that she would much rather stay at home.

There was also the question of the phone; while her first thought had been to escape from it, she'd since remembered that the Chief Inspector wanted her to take the call. Mrs

Bedale would have to give any callers the Teals' number.

The drive from north-west to north-east Shillingham should have been a simple matter of following the ring-road. Today, however, it was made frustrating by the vagaries of Sunday drivers, and by the time they arrived Monica was hot, sticky and short-tempered, with her migraine simmering nicely. However, as she'd expected, her sister's home was an oasis of cool welcome, with discreetly hidden fans blowing through the rooms, and by the time she'd held her wrists under the cold tap in the cloakroom, she'd recovered her equilibrium.

She was surprised to find the Marlows there; another instance of Eloise not warning her what kind of gathering to expect. Claudia was extremely chic in a new Randall Tovey dress, a caramel linen that beautifully offset her slight tan. But Monica's initially approving glance also detected strain; the hand holding her glass shook slightly, the other gripped her handbag. Harry also seemed subdued, and Monica sensed there'd been words before leaving home.

'Sorry our young aren't here for you,' Eloise was saying to Abbie, handing her a long cold drink. 'This was all a last-minute idea, as you'll have gathered, and they had other plans.'

Claudia saw her daughter droop, and ached for her. She could have stayed home to revise, after all. Personally, she wished they'd all stayed home; she was hating every minute of this. Whenever she'd been here before, even as recently as last Tuesday, she'd felt happy and relaxed. Now, for no reason she could pinpoint, it had all changed. Yet the change, she knew, was within her. It was as though she watched them all through distorting mirrors. Eloise had turned from Abbie to Harry.

'All set for the Private View?' she asked him, offering a dish of nuts.

'As much as we can be at this stage. The replies are starting to flood in at long last.'

'I hope you can find room for Theo; he wasn't invited, but he'd love to come.'

'Oh Lord, I'm sorry—someone always gets overlooked at these things. I'll have a word with my typist and make sure he's put on the list.'

'Will you be helping with the hanging, Claudia?'

Claudia started to find herself addressed, but Harry was answering for her, an edge to his voice.

'No, no, that's not her scene. Claudia prefers to swan in when all the hard work's been done and the bubbly's on hand, don't you, darling?'

Claudia said tightly, 'I shan't be helping, no. I'm lunching in Broadminster on Tuesday and don't know what time I'll be back.'

'You do enough behind the scenes anyway,' Eloise said tactfully. 'But if you do need any help, Harry, I could spare an hour or two.'

'Thanks, I might take you up on that.'

Into the awkward silence, Monica said, 'It's very noble of you, Eloise, to have us for Sunday lunch, specially when you've no help with the meal. I don't suppose your caterers were available at short notice?'

Her sister laughed. 'I've a confession to make: one reason why I've invited you all is that we had a dinner-party last night and there's quite a lot of food left over. Though the main reason, naturally, is that we wanted to see you!'

Monica smiled. 'We're not proud, particularly when it comes to "Home Cooking's" specialties. I thought, incidentally, that they excelled themselves on Tuesday.'

'Yes, they do very well.' Eloise rose to her feet. 'If everyone's ready, shall we go through?'

As they moved into the hall, Monica found Justin at her side.

'Are you all right? You look rather pale.'

'A migraine hovering, I'm afraid. It's like an oven outside.'

'Perhaps something to eat will help.'

But Monica knew resignedly that once it had got this far, there was no deflecting the headache. Already the bright colours in Eloise's dress were hurting her eyes.

The meal progressed. Monica made an effort to eat the delicious cold food spread before her, but her appetite had gone. Claudia, she noted, was doing little better. Poor Eloise, her 'finishing up' party was letting her down.

A mint sorbet spiked with crème-de-menthe ended the meal and they returned to the sitting-room, where conversation continued in a desultory fashion over coffee and, later, tea. Though she longed for the dimness of drawn curtains and the quiet of her own room, Monica had no energy to make a move. It was left to her mother, who, perhaps of all of them, was the one who'd enjoyed the occasion without reservation, to mention the time.

'We mustn't outstay our welcome,' she remarked, 'and you're looking a bit peaky, darling. Didn't your headache lift?'

'Unfortunately not.'

Justin said quickly. 'Look, I'll drive you home. One of the boys can bring your car round tomorrow.'

'No, really, I'll be all right.'

'No arguments. You're not in a fit state to drive, by the look of you.'

It was too much effort to protest, and in any case the thought of someone else driving was like a load being lifted from her. Among the murmurs of concern, she allowed herself to be escorted to the car and helped into the back seat.

'What an end to a day out!' she said shakily. 'I do apologize.'

'Nonsense. We didn't realize how badly you were feeling, though I should have known, since Eloise has the same trouble.'

Monica rested her head against the back seat and thankfully closed her eyes. The swaying motion of the car made her nauseous and she could feel sweat pricking at her skin. Still, the ordeal would soon be over and she could go to bed.

When they reached North Park, Justin insisted on escorting them up the path and waiting till Monica had inserted her key and swung the door open.

'Now you're sure you'll be all right? Would you like me to phone the doctor?'

She shook her head. 'He'd only advise rest and darkness. Thanks, Justin, you very probably saved my life.'

'Theo will bring your car round before he goes to work. Straight to bed, now, and take care. Goodbye, Maude. It was lovely to see you.'

As Monica pushed the door closed behind them, Mrs Bedale came out of the kitchen. 'Did you get the phone call, Miss Tovey?'

Monica halted, an enervating flood of heat pouring over her. 'What phone call?'

'The gentleman who rang before. I gave him Mrs Teal's number, like you said.'

'Oh God,' said Monica through dry lips. 'No, I didn't. I have a migraine, Mrs Bedale; I shan't want any supper, I'm going straight to bed.'

And leaving the two women in the hall, she dragged herself up the stairs.

Had the police managed to trace the call? She was incapable of phoning them to find out. Well, she'd done all she could; if he'd wanted, he could have contacted her at the Teals'. Perhaps he didn't intend to speak to her at all, but just to leave messages to frighten her. Though as far as she knew he hadn't even done that; she'd not specifically asked, but she wasn't going downstairs again to check.

Suddenly aware that she was going to vomit, Monica turned and staggered towards the bathroom.

'Not one of our more successful occasions, darling,' Justin said drily on his return. 'Poor Monica in obvious pain and sparks flying between Claudia and Harry. That's unusual; I wonder what had happened?'

'No doubt even the most devoted couples have rows sometimes.'

He turned at her tone of voice. 'You think they are devoted? I don't know that I'd have put it so strongly.'

'Goodness, Justin, how should I know? They've always seemed perfectly happy.'

'Yes.' He paused. 'You know, I was thinking only the other day that it says a lot for Harry that he's still our friend. We treated him pretty badly, didn't we?'

'The selfishness of young love!'

'I sometimes wonder if he still wishes things had turned out differently.'

'Oh, he's very fond of Claudia, and he adores Abbie. They're fine; it was probably some little disagreement they'd had before they came which they'd not had time to talk through. I did like her dress,' Eloise continued, flipping through the pages of the colour supplement. 'I must ask Monica which designer it was.'

Justin took the hint that his wife didn't want to probe any deeper into their friends' affairs. It was some time later that he realized she'd bypassed his comment on Harry's feelings towards herself.

The ringing of the phone bored into her head like a pneumatic drill. Blindly she reached out for it, more intent on stopping the noise than discovering who was calling. But as a gruff, hesitant voice said, 'Miss Tovey?' she was suddenly, icily, awake. He'd caught up with her at last.

She hitched herself up on one elbow. 'Yes?'

'I'm the bloke you saw that night. By the van.'

'I know.'

'When I read what they found in the back, I—'

'*Read* it?'

'That's right; I'd no idea, I swear it!'

She said whitely, 'But if that's true, how—?'

'I'd been visiting a friend, see, and missed the last bus. Well, I was in a fair old stew, 'cos I had to be at the depot by five. I tried hitching but no one would stop, so I started to walk, and then I saw this van in a lay-by. It was—'

'Wait!' Monica interrupted, picking her way through the irrelevancies. 'Are you trying to tell me you didn't kill those boys?'

''Course I didn't! I'd no idea they were there! Fair makes my flesh crawl, thinking about it.'

Were the police getting this? 'Then why in the name of heaven didn't you come forward and explain?'

'There were reasons. But—'

'Look here, young man.' The invalid was giving way to the magistrate. 'Do you realize that not only have you hindered police inquiries, you've also given me an extremely worrying few days?'

'Yes, sorry about that. I tried to phone—'

'Only twice. Why didn't you ring again?'

'I was out of the country, wasn't I, driving a load to Belgium. Left five o'clock Friday morning and got back dinner-time today. I did phone earlier but you were out again.'

'I know,' she said weakly, her anger beginning to evaporate in enormous relief. 'But never mind me, why didn't you tell the police? By phone if you didn't want to call in, just to let them know they were looking for the wrong man?'

'They can trace calls, even from public phone-boxes. They'd have nabbed me for nicking the van.'

'But you'll have to see them. You might have valuable information.'

'I haven't—I just said! I don't know nothing.'

'Nevertheless, you must go.' She reached for the bedside pad. 'What's your name and address?'

Her voice must have held authority, because to her surprise he gave them: Frank Andrews, 3 Calder's Close. They could both be false, but it was a starting-point.

'I'm sure they'll go easy on you,' she added. 'You will see them, won't you? Tomorrow? Ask for Mr Webb, at Carrington Street.'

He didn't reply, and she said urgently, 'Promise me you will.'

'All right,' he said sulkily, 'but they'd better believe me about the van. I didn't have to phone, you know,' he added, with a burst of righteous indignation.

'I know, and I'm very grateful that you did. I've not enjoyed the past week.'

'No, I reckon not. Sorry.'

'Mr Webb, at Carrington Street,' she repeated, hoping the forcefulness of her request would last until the next morning.

As he rang off she swung her feet to he floor and waited for the dizziness to subside. Where had she put the Chief Inspector's number? The police should now know as much as she did, but she wanted confirmation of the fact.

As it happened, Webb was also in bed at ten o'clock that Sunday, but he was not alone. Swearing softly, he answered the insistent ringing of the telephone.

Hannah, lying beside him, gathered it was the man tapping Monica's phone. She'd called her friend twice over the last few days to see if the mystery caller'd rung back, and knew the strain she was under.

David put the phone down and turned back to her. 'As you'll have gathered, the bloke's just been on again. And, would you believe, he's insisting he's not the murderer after all. How do you like that? Your friend Miss Tovey got a name and address out of him and made him promise to come to the station in the morning.'

'Good for Monica. But if he's not—'

The phone interrupted her with shrill insistence. With a grimace Webb lifted it again, to find Monica herself on the line.

'Sorry, my love,' he said as he replaced it, 'she's naturally a bit jumpy and she needs someone to talk to. I'll have to go over.'

'Of course. You think he's telling the truth, about not being the murderer?'

'From what I heard, it sounds genuine. Just our luck, when he finally materializes.' He was already out of bed and pulling on his clothes. 'She says she's not too good— migraine—so I'll be as quick as I can. You'll stay, won't you?'

'Oh, I think so. I'm too lazy to dress and go back downstairs.'

'Fine, then I'll be even quicker!' He bent to kiss her swiftly before hurrying out of the door, knotting his tie as he went.

He hadn't yet met Miss Tovey, Webb reflected, as he started up the car. Possibly that was remiss of him, but Dawson had given him a full report and he had to delegate sometimes. The only sight he'd had of her was when she went down the path after dining with Hannah, and the impression he'd received was of a small woman, though it was hard to gauge heights from the second floor.

As it happened, the impression had been correct. She opened the door to him in a pale silk housecoat, apologizing for it as she did so. 'As I mentioned, I wasn't well earlier, and went to bed soon after six. Consequently when the phone rang, it took me a few minutes to collect myself.'

'You sound to have done admirably,' he said, following her into the drawing-room. Though she was quite small, she had a sense of presence which authority at work and on the Bench had no doubt nurtured. For the rest, her fair curly hair was beginning to fade to grey, but her eyes were clear and candid and could have been those of a young girl.

Monica for her part was sizing up her visitor, whom she'd seen in the distance once or twice at Court. Close to, she saw a tall, lean man—in his late forties, probably—with plentiful brown hair, a hard-looking mouth and rather bleak grey eyes. Not someone she'd care to cross, she decided.

His manner was considerate, though, and he led her gently through her conversation with Frank Andrews, eliciting all the information she had with the minimum amount of questioning. It took a surprisingly short time.

'Your men did get everything?' she asked anxiously.

'Yes, but I haven't had a transcript yet. Your account has been most helpful.'

'And you will give him a chance to turn up voluntarily?'

'Oh yes. Someone will be watching the address he gave, but we'll play it carefully and wait to see what he does.'

She nodded, satisfied.

'I'm very grateful for your help, Miss Tovey,' he added as he took his leave. 'Especially since you're under the weather. I hope your headache clears up soon.'

'Thank you; I think the worst is over now. I'll be interested to know what happens tomorrow.'

'So shall I!' His sudden smile lit his face, surprising her by its attractiveness. 'Don't worry, I'll keep you informed.'

A man of many parts, Chief Inspector Webb. As Monica went back to her room, her earlier euphoric relief settled into comforting reality. It was over; the frightening memory of the man's face beneath her window, the worry about the unknown caller, the shadows in the mews that were suddenly so menacing. Her life as it had been a week ago had been handed back to her, and she was inordinately grateful.

It was only as she was falling asleep that she remembered her visit to church that morning. The Almighty had fulfilled his part of the bargain; it was now up to her to stick to hers.

CHAPTER 9

Webb was at his desk by 8.30 the next morning, and at 8.45 the tail he had put on Frank Andrews reported a man answering his description had just left the house. He was being followed, and was driving in the direction of Carrington Street.

'John Baker's still being hassled about that plane,' Crombie remarked, breaking into Webb's musings. 'The Badderleys mentioned it when they collected their property. You remember they reported it at the time of the break-in.'

Webb had a mental picture of the unpleasant woman with red toenails. 'So you said.'

'They wondered if we'd found out any more.'

'What time did they see it?'

'Just before eleven. It gave them quite a fright—they thought it was going to come down on top of them. Of course, it landed only a mile or two down the road.'

'Yes,' Webb said slowly. 'I wonder—'

The phone interrupted him. 'Someone at the desk asking for you, sir,' reported the station sergeant. 'Name of Andrews.'

'I'll be right down.'

He dropped the phone, strode rapidly through the outer office and ran down the stairs. Frank Andrews had proved so elusive, he wouldn't feel he had him till he was sitting across the table from him.

The man who turned warily to face him was just as he'd imagined—a tribute to Miss Tovey's description. Medium height, red hair, probably the same jeans and jacket. Add to that the white face that frequently goes with red hair, and pale blue, apprehensive eyes.

'Mr Andrews?'

'That's right.'

'Chief Inspector Webb. If you'd like to come through?'

Andrews cast one longing look back at the front entrance, then meekly preceded Webb into the interview room where Jackson was already waiting. So far, so good.

The man was clearly nervous; sweat lined his upper lip and his shoulders were tense. So should he bloody well be nervous, after all the trouble he'd caused. Nevertheless, he'd be more use if he relaxed. 'Tea? Coffee?' Webb asked pleasantly.

'Oh—tea. Ta very much.' Webb nodded to Jackson, who went in search of it. They sat in silence till he returned with a tin tray and three mugs.

'Now, Mr Andrews,' Webb began, when the mugs had been distributed, 'we're hoping you'll be able to clear up a few things for us. It's a pity you weren't able to come in earlier.'

Andrews flicked him a wary glance. 'I've been abroad,' he said. Webb let that pass for the moment, and the man's full name and address were duly noted. He gave the latter reluctantly.

'You won't be going round there, will you? Only the wife doesn't know anything about all this.'

'We'll be discreet,' Webb said. 'Right, then; we'd like you to tell us exactly what happened. From the beginning.'

Andrews licked his lips, took a gulp of tea, and began. 'Well, it was like I told the lady. My car was in for service, so I took the bus. I wasn't watching the time—'

'Where had you gone?'

The man hesitated. 'To visit a friend.'

'Name and address?'

Andrews threw him an agonized look. 'Do I have to?'

'I'm afraid so.'

'Miss Jennifer Stevens, three-four-seven Chipping Claydon Road.'

'Go on.'

'Well, as I say, I didn't realize the time and the upshot was I left it too late and missed the last bus. And I *had* to get back. The wife was expecting me—she thought I was at the pub—and I had to be at the depot for five the next morning.'

The name and address of the transport firm were written down.

'I tried hitching a lift,' Andrews continued, 'but the miserable buggers wouldn't stop so I started walking. And as I was passing the lay-by this lorry went by and its headlights picked up the van. Well, I thought my luck was in; if someone had stopped for a break, I reckoned I could cadge a lift. I went over, but the van was empty. Then I saw the keys in the ignition, which seemed odd.'

Andrews took another drink of tea. 'I expected the driver any minute so I hung around but no one came. Time was going on, and after a while I began to wonder if it had been abandoned. That'd account for the keys being left in it. I was pretty het up by this time, so I decided to get in and try to start it. If it went OK, I'd borrow it to get home, and run it back next day. Honest to God, I'd have done that. What use is a clapped-out old van to me, anyway?'

Presumably it was a rhetorical question. At any rate Webb treated it as such, and after a moment Andrews went on, wiping the sweat off his face with the sleeve of his jacket.

'But half way back the bloody thing started playing up, and it finally ground to a halt outside that house.'

'If you were making for the far side of Shillingham,' Webb interrupted, 'what were you doing in North Park? The main road runs straight into town.'

Andrews flushed. 'Yeah, but as I was going under the motorway I saw one of your lot just ahead, blue lights and all. I wasn't going near him in my borrowed van, now was I? So when he kept on along the main road I veered off to the right, which took me up the hill by the park. I reckoned by the time I'd filtered back to the main road, I'd have lost him.'

As simple as that. 'Go on.'

'That's about it. I tried to get the van going, but it wouldn't budge so I got out. And then I looked up and saw this face at the window staring down at me. Fair gave me a turn, I can tell you. So I legged it off down the hill.'

'And your good intentions of returning the van went by the board?'

'I wasn't going up there in broad daylight with a can of petrol in my hand. Not to a posh area like that. I reckoned if the owner wanted it back, he'd keep an eye open for reports of abandoned vehicles.

'But then—' he swallowed convulsively—'on Wednesday night it said in the *News* two bodies had been found in it. Strewth, that was all I needed! I swear I never slept a wink. All I could think of was that woman watching me—and she'd a good view, because I was under the lamp—and her thinking it was me that had done it. There'd be a photo-fit in the paper, and the wife would see it.'

'How did you find out who the lady was?'

'Checked the house in the register at the library. Simple enough. And the name was the same as the shop. I tried to phone her a couple of times, but I had to go to Belgium first thing Friday, so yesterday was the next chance I got.'

'You realize you put her through a very worrying time?'

'Well, I'm sorry, but I had to choose my time, with the wife in the house.'

'Right, Mr Andrews, thank you. If you'll read through and sign the statement Sergeant Jackson's taken down, that'll be all for the moment.'

'Back to square one, eh, Guv?' Jackson commented, following Webb upstairs after seeing Andrews out.

'Yes, the field's wide open again. All we've got now is that car parked under the trees.' But at least one point had been cleared up; the murderer had not after all been so foolhardy as to drive off in his victim's van. That had worried him all along.

'Come into my office, Ken, and let's talk this through.' He pushed open the door, and Crombie looked up from his desk.

'Here's that list of the Whites' customers, Dave. Those known to have business dealings with Miss Tovey have been highlighted, but no doubt she knows a lot of the others as well.'

'I doubt if it's relevant now, Alan; we've established that the van stopping outside her house was pure chance. By the way—' he sat down at his desk—'before Andrews arrived, we were talking about that plane and I think it's time we gave it a bit more thought.'

'Don't tell me you're considering a connection after all?' Webb's original reaction to the idea still rankled.

'There could be a tenuous one. We now know it was the Whites who did the Badderley house, and that the plane landed nearby at about the same time. Also, we suspect the lads met their death through a blackmail attempt that went wrong. Why else all that excitement about keeping a rendezvous in a lay-by?'

'So?' Crombie still wasn't sticking his neck out.

'So, Alan,' Webb said deliberately, 'it could well be you were on to something after all. Suppose the twins saw the plane land and stopped to investigate? And spotted something—or someone—they considered worth following up?'

Jackson, who'd silently taken a seat alongside Webb's

desk during this exchange, gave a small cough, and as the two senior officers glanced at him, said diffidently, 'I was talking to Joe Casey the other day. Another consignment of heroin's hit the streets; he narrowly missed a transaction at the Whistle Stop.'

'You mean the plane probably landed it? I know that's what the Drug Squad have been working on, but—'

'Yes, Guv, but I was reading Bob Dawson's interview with the Hargreaves. One of the reasons they threw the lads out was that they were smoking pot.'

Webb's eyes narrowed. 'Go on.'

'I know there was no evidence of the habit at the PM, but because they'd kicked it themselves doesn't mean they weren't pushing it.'

'You've a point there, Ken. Come to that, even if they weren't involved, they might have recognized someone who supplied them in the old days. His name could even be here, among their customers. Let's have a quick run-through.'

He glanced down at the list. 'We'll start with the ones who know Miss Tovey: Carruthers, France and Studley, dental surgeons, 24 Kimberley Road; Alexander's Hairdressing Salon, 42 East Parade; National Bank, King Street branch, Manager Mr G. A. Latimer (personal and business accounts); Rayner & Teal, wine importers, 39 Duke Street.' He looked up with a grin. 'Mr Teal's another magistrate, isn't he? Not a promising bunch for international drug-smugglers, you must admit.'

'Randall Tovey's on the list too,' Crombie reminded him. 'How about Miss Tovey herself?'

Ignoring both Webbb's and Jackson's surprise, he went on, warming to his theme. 'Andrews came upon the deserted van about eleven-thirty and didn't reach North Park with it till midnight. If the murder took place at eleven, the killer could have been safely tucked up in bed by then.'

Webb looked at him disbelievingly. 'You're not seriously suggesting Miss Tovey's running a dope ring?'

'It's feasible. She's plenty of wealthy contacts; the habit's not limited to the down-and-outs, as we know only too well.

And if she *had* met the plane, the Whites would certainly
have recognized her; they'd been up before her often
enough.'

'But if Miss Tovey topped them, she'd have recognized
their van when it appeared outside her house.'

'Perhaps she did,' Jackson said, entering into the spirit
of the argument. 'But she wouldn't have let on, would she?
Not a clever lady like that. She'd have done exactly what
an innocent person would do; wait to see if someone was
coming back for it, and when they didn't, get on to us.'

'It'd have given her one hell of a shock, turning up on
her doorstep,' Crombie said reflectively.

'Come to that,' put in Webb, 'whoever the killer is, he'd
have had one hell of a shock when the van appeared in
North Park. Must have done his nut wondering how and
why it arrived there from the lay-by. Anyway, back to the
list: what other customers had they got?'

He ran his eye down the page, reading out names at
random. Punjabi Gardens Restaurant—Hong Kong Restaurant—Carlton Gallery—'

'They've got an exhibition there this week,' Crombie
cut in. 'I saw a notice in the newsagent's. Wednesday to
Saturday, I think.'

'I know, I intend to look in if I get the chance.' Webb,
an amateur artist and cartoonist, was quite familiar with
the Carlton. In fact, he'd an eye on a print he hoped to buy
for Hannah's birthday.

'Well, we'll have to see the whole lot. What'll be interesting is to find out how many of them knew the Whites were
their window-cleaners.'

'Surely they all did, Guv,' Jackson interpolated. 'You can
hardly miss a face at your window!'

'Oh, they probably knew them by sight,' Crombie
agreed, 'but could they have put a name to them? I've
no idea what *our* window-cleaner is called. I bet half the
Whites' customers still don't realize that the "bodies in
the van", as the press call them, are the same lads that
did their windows.'

'No harm in telling them, then,' Webb said, putting the list in his desk drawer and getting to his feet. 'I promised Miss Tovey I'd let her know if Andrews turned up. Instead of phoning, I'll go in and see her, and ask about the Whites at the same time. Not to mention the current price for cocaine. Ready, Ken?'

In the car on the way to East Parade, Jackson said tentatively, 'The DI wasn't serious about Miss Tovey, was he, Guv? I mean, I know I joined in, but it was only for the sake of argument. I didn't really believe it.'

'It's a possibility, nothing more. Trouble with cases like this, you can't completely discount anyone.'

'But her a magistrate and all—'

Webb shrugged. 'Could be a good cover. I'll tell you this, though, Ken. Having met the lady, I can't really see her in the rôle of drug-smuggler and murderer.' Especially since she's a friend of Hannah's, he added mockingly to himself. With which unprofessional proviso, he got out of the car outside Randall Tovey and walked into its foyer.

She was looking a lot better than the previous evening. Webb wondered how much of the improvement was due to the departure of the migraine and how much to her conversation with Frank Andrews.

'Did he turn up?' she asked eagerly, as soon as she'd shaken Webb's hand.

'Yes, ma'am, we got the full story.'

'And you think he's genuine?'

'I'd say so. We're checking times with his girlfriend and the transport firm he works for, but it seems to tie in.'

'Well, that is a relief.'

'Yes. However, we've still the real murderer to find. Miss Tovey, were you aware that the White brothers cleaned the windows here?'

She stared at him for a moment. 'The windows? Oh, I see. I did know, yes, though I'd forgotten. Is it important?'

'It could be, if they were killed because of something they saw in the course of their work.'

She smiled a little. 'All they'd have seen here, Chief Inspector, would be ladies trying to squeeze into a dress one size too small. And since the windows are frosted in the changing-rooms, they wouldn't have seen much of that.'

The phone rang on her desk. 'Would you excuse me for a moment? Hello? Oh, Justin.' Webb and Jackson exchanged a quick glance. 'Yes, thank you, much better. And please thank Theo for bringing the car round.'

There was a silence broken only by the murmur from the telephone. Then she said, 'Has she? I am sorry; perhaps it's the weather . . . This evening? Well, yes, I should think so . . . No, really, I've fully recovered, though to be safe I'll avoid shellfish and red wine . . . Yes, I've met Monsieur Clériot . . . Did he? How kind of him. Very well, Justin, I'll be ready at seven-thirty . . . Not at all, I'll be glad to.'

She put the phone back, and smiled at the two men sitting expressionlessly opposite. 'Sorry about that. My brother-in-law wants me to act as hostess for him this evening. It seems it's my sister's turn to have a migraine.'

Webb said quickly, 'Your brother-in-law?'

'That's right, Justin Teal. You may know him, he sits on the Bench.'

'I know of him, yes, but I didn't realize you were related.' He paused, wondering how best to phrase what he wanted to know. 'It's a case of business entertaining, is it? This evening?'

She looked surprised at his interest, but answered readily enough. 'Yes; a lot of his suppliers have difficulty with English, and since I speak French and Italian it comes in very useful.'

'With your brother-in-law being in the wine business, he must take fairly regular trips abroad?'

'Of course.' She paused. 'Forgive me, Chief Inspector, but why this sudden interest in my brother-in-law? Was he a customer of the Whites too?'

Webb smiled a little shamefacedly. 'Actually, he was. As were quite a lot of business premises in this area.'

'And you really think the twins might have seen something they shouldn't have?'

'We've yet to find a motive for their murder, Miss Tovey. When we do, we might have a clue as to their murderer.' He rose to his feet, motioning Jackson to do likewise. 'I hope you enjoy your dinner this evening.'

'I expect to; we're going to The Gables, at Frecklemarsh.'

Webb paused. 'Does Mr Pendrick still own it?'

'Yes indeed. Do you know him?'

'We met a few years ago.' When he was suspected of murdering his wife. 'Give him my best wishes,' he added, smiling to himself as he pictured Pendrick's reception of them.

'I shall.' She came round her desk to open the door for them. 'Goodbye, Chief Inspector. Miss Lancing will see you downstairs.' She nodded to one of the assistants, who dutifully came forward, and the two men followed her in solemn procession between the rails of brightly coloured dresses and down the stairs.

'Well, Ken, what do you make of that?' Webb asked as they reached the pavement. 'Regular contacts with people from the continent—which both Teal and Miss Tovey have —could be a cover for all kinds of things.'

'Sinister foreigners, you mean, Guv?' Jackson asked. 'Perhaps we should be looking for Fu Manchu!' And he ducked Webb's cuff with a grin.

'What we are going to do now, my lad, is go out and see this Preston family. The Whites were with them immediately before the Trubshaws. Let's find out if they smoked pot while they were there.'

The Bridgefield council estate lay a few miles outside Shillingham on the Marlton road. It had been built only six years but already had a shabby, dilapidated air, with broken fences, overgrown hedges and graffiti scrawled on a wall. Three or four small children were playing on tricycles, swooping on and off the pavement, but there was no other sign of life. Presumably most of the inhabitants were at work.

Webb and Jackson got out of their car in front of the Prestons' house, and, ignoring the children's wide-eyed stares, walked up the path and knocked at the door. There was a long pause and then it was opened by a girl of sixteen or seventeen, who regarded them suspiciously.

'We're looking for Mr or Mrs Preston,' Webb said pleasantly.

'They're not in.'

'You're Miss Preston?' A nod. 'Could we have a word with you, then? We're from Shillingham CID, Chief Inspector Webb and Sergeant Jackson.'

He produced his identification, but she barely glanced at it. 'I knew you were the fuzz. It sticks out a mile.'

'May we come in for a moment? We'd like to ask you a few questions about the White twins.'

The effect of his words was surprising, because the girl's eyes filled with tears.

He said more gently, 'We don't want to upset you, miss, but you might be able to help.'

She turned away without speaking, but since she left the door open, they took it as an invitation and followed her inside. The kitchen into which she had retreated overlooked a rough patch of garden. In one corner the chassis of an old pram lay abandoned, its wheels no doubt now gracing some other form of transport.

'Could we have your name, miss?'

'Dolores,' the girl answered with a sniff.

'You obviously remember the Whites,' Webb began, but she cut him short.

'Be surprising if I didn't, when we had an Indian with them only last month.' The tears welled up again and spilled down her cheek.

'You've kept in touch with them?' That was better than he could have hoped for.

'Yeh. Damien mostly, my brother.'

'He's not in, I suppose?' She shook her head.

'How long did they live here?'

'A couple of years.'

'And why did they leave?'

'Wanted to be nearer the football club.'

'There was no—trouble—of any kind?'

'No, of course not. They was like part of the family. Mum cried when they went.'

It was another example of the opposing feelings the twins had aroused: suspicion and distrust in Mr Hargreaves and Mrs Trubshaw, genuine affection in her husband and the Prestons.

'And that meal you had was the last time you saw them. Can you remember when it was?'

'After the Oxbury match.'

'Which was?'

'The last Saturday in April, I think. We celebrated at the clubhouse, then went on to the Punjabi Gardens.'

It was the second time that name had come up today. Any significance?

'How often did you all meet?'

'Damien saw them more than me, but they came here to supper sometimes. They were great.' Her voice trembled.

'Dolores—' Webb used her first name in the hope of softening the questions which were to follow. 'Do you know if they ever smoked pot?'

She looked at him sharply, and he added, 'You won't be getting anyone in trouble. It's just that we're trying to find out who killed them, and that could be a lead.'

She said slowly, 'They did a bit, when they first came, but Mum didn't like it, so they stopped. It didn't matter to them, one way or the other.'

'Any other kind of drugs?'

'No.'

'Did you ever hear them mention drugs? Anyone they knew on them, something like that?'

'Rob told me someone he was at school with died of an

overdose. It shook him quite a bit. He said it was a mug's game.'

'Did he make any other comment?'

'Only that he'd like to get his hands on the bastard that sold it him.'

Not dealers themselves, then, but perhaps a motive for blackmailing those who were.

'Do you know anyone who didn't like the twins—had it in for them?'

'Only rival fans. There used to be punch-ups sometimes.'

'Did your brother go with them to matches?' A Preston had not been mentioned among the gang.

'No, he's not into football. He goes dog-racing.'

'One more thing, Dolores, then we'll go. This may be painful for you, but could you tell us the first thing that came into your head when you heard they'd been killed?'

'That I was glad they went together.'

'They were that close?'

'Yeh. It was spooky.'

'But you'd no idea who could have killed them?'

'No. It would only have made sense after a match.' She knuckled her eyes in a touchingly childish gesture. 'I hope you get who did it,' she said.

CHAPTER 10

George Latimer believed firmly that there was no such thing as a free dinner. On the other hand, evenings at home were stultifying and Monica, as he'd learned at lunch-time, was playing hostess to Justin yet again. He intended to put a stop to that once they were married. If they ever did marry.

He sighed; she'd seemed to need him the other night after her anonymous phone calls, but her dependence had been short-lived. The danger was now over; that was why she'd telephoned, and the measure of relief with which he'd heard the news was in proportion to the anxiety he'd felt.

All the same, he thought ruefully, it had been good to feel he was needed. And in the stress of the moment, she *had* agreed to a weekend away. He'd remind her of that, next time they spoke.

Now, though, he had other things on his mind, such as how, after a good meal, impartiality could be maintained regarding the increased loan which he was sure was behind the invitation.

At least, he thought as he got into the car, his clients had drawn the line at taking him to The Gables, where Monica was bound this evening. No doubt there were grades of restaurant for entertaining possibly compliant bank managers. Someone should do a sociological survey on it.

Frecklemarsh, a village eight miles south-west of Shillingham, owed its fame to The Gables, a small but highly regarded hotel renowned for its cuisine. It was a popular choice for wedding receptions and twenty-first parties, but its clientele was mainly drawn from businessmen on expense accounts who wished to impress foreign clients, and by wealthy families wanting a base from which to explore the Broadshire countryside.

The ambience was that of a country house, with genuine antiques, comfortable chairs and, in winter, log fires burning in the grates, and the relaxed atmosphere was due in no small measure to its proprietor, Oliver Pendrick.

He made it a practice to greet all his clients personally, and was as usual in the hall when Justin and Monica arrived with the two Frenchmen, father and son, who were their guests.

'Mr Teal!' Pendrick came forward, holding out his hand. 'Good to see you! And Miss Tovey. How's your mother?'

Monica watched with admiration as Justin introduced the Clériots and the proprietor slipped easily into French, immediately putting them at ease. He was, she knew, a widower, a tall, well-built man in his early fifties, with thick red-brown hair hardly touched with grey, and deepset eyes.

'How's Henry?' Justin was asking, as Pendrick himself led them through to the restaurant.

'Doing very well. He's spending a year at the Georges V and loving every moment of it.' He stopped at their table and pulled out a chair for Monica. 'Enjoy your meal!' And he left them to attend to the next arrivals.

'Henri is the son?' Monsieur Clériot inquired in French, as a waiter shook out a napkin and laid it across his knees.

'Yes; following the family tradition, as you'll gather.'

'The Georges V is a formidable training-ground!'

The pleasantries over, the talk turned almost immediately to business and Monica, steering clear of the more exotic dishes out of deference to her migraine, allowed her thoughts to wander. How wonderful it had been to drive here this evening without the knowledge that a police guard was of necessity following her, to walk fearlessly without looking back over her shoulder. That anxious time had lasted only five days, but the memory of it would, she knew, be longlasting. At least it had taught her to take nothing for granted.

Half-listening to the soft cadences of French, she thought back to that morning and the Chief Inspector's visit. Why had the fact that Justin travelled abroad interested him? For that matter, what did he suspect the White twins had seen which was to lead to their death? Who else's windows had they cleaned?

She conjured them up in her mind—clipped blond hair, blue eyes, the cocky, defiant stance. They'd been so *young*; she'd hoped to be able to reform them in time, but had not been given the chance. More importantly, neither had they.

Justin claimed her attention with a query, and she re-entered the general conversation.

'It was my fault; I shouldn't have asked you.' Eloise lay back on the chaise-longue, her body barred with shadow as the evening sun filtered through venetian blinds.

'It's never been a problem before,' Harry replied. They were in the upper room at the Carlton Gallery, surrounded by stacked canvases waiting to be hung the next day.

'But she resented the short notice, you said.'

'Oh, it was a combination of things; having the lunch all prepared, looking forward to a lazy day—'

'Yes, I should have known better than ring so late. The point was, of course, that I hadn't intended to invite you; I'd phoned Mother first thing. But then, well, the pressure was building up. I needed to see you, and didn't stop to think.'

'You couldn't have known Claudia'd react like that.'

'You don't think it's serious, though?'

'I don't know; I keep wondering if she could have heard something.'

'What, for heaven's sake, since no one else knows? We've always been so careful.'

'We're not being too careful now, meeting this evening. Specially since you're supposed to be prostrate with a migraine.'

She shrugged her bony shoulders. 'Justin knows that's an excuse. My noble sister stepped into the breach as usual.'

'What about *her* migraine? That was genuine enough.'

'Better now, apparently. Oh, and that man she'd seen by the van phoned her last night. And guess what? He's not the murderer after all!'

Harry retrieved his shirt which had slid to the floor and tossed it on to a nearby chair. 'Well, he would say that, wouldn't he?'

'The police seem to believe him. Apparently he found the van in a lay-by and stole it.'

'And got more than he bargained for? That should teach him a lesson.'

'So they're back to square one on the real killer, and Justin's still worried about it. He thinks it's too much of a coincidence, the bodies being left where they were, when Monica'd had dealings with them.'

She looked up at him and trailed a long finger down his back. 'And talking of Justin, he suddenly remarked last night on what a good friend you were.'

'My God! What brought that on?'

'I don't know; he said he'd been thinking how badly he and I treated you all those years ago, and that it said a lot for you that we were still friends.' She paused. 'He also made some comment about wondering if you still regretted what had happened.'

'That's a bit near the bone, particularly coming on top of Claudia's wobbler. Perhaps we should play it down for a while, once tomorrow's over.'

'Is everything ready? For tomorrow?'

'Except for those.' He indicated the unhung paintings.

'You do think it'll go off all right?'

'No reason why it shouldn't. Heaven knows, enough planning has gone into it. Even,' he added with a smile, 'to the extent of booking Home Cooking for the refreshments. So in the meantime—' he turned towards her—'if we're going to have to cool it for a while, let's make the most of this evening.'

They were a pleasant enough couple, the Davidsons, and George was quite enjoying himself. The husband, a bluff rather hearty man, was a bit of a social climber, and George knew well enough that the loan around which he'd been skirting so dextrously all evening was intended to offset public school fees for his sons. However, he was good company, and he'd splashed out on an excellent bottle of wine; another point which required finesse when entertaining one's bank manager.

Mrs Davidson was clearly nervous, picking at her food and anxiously watching her husband for any sign that she wasn't fulfilling her duties as hostess. Meanwhile George, with no particular worries on his mind, was savouring his meal. They had reached the cheese course when, as he casually glanced across the room, he caught sight of Jeremy Teal.

Although he'd never discussed them with her, George shared Monica's distrust of her nephews. Too plausible by half; if they worked for him, he'd keep them on a pretty tight rein. He craned his neck, trying to see if the decorative

and empty-headed Primrose was also present. She was not;
Jeremy's companions were two dark, sallow-skinned men,
who appeared to be deep in conversation with him.

What was the boy up to? Had he been alone himself,
George would have been tempted to stroll over to their table
simply to see Jeremy's reaction: because something in the
set of his shoulders spoke of tension, and quite possibly an
unwillingness to be spotted by anyone he knew.

'More wine, Mr Latimer?' Davidson held up the bottle
invitingly.

'No, thank you, I'm driving. It was very good, though. I
must watch out for that label.'

'No doubt it was supplied by Rayner & Teal. They seem
to have this area nicely sewn up, and good luck to them.
Aren't they related to the Tovey family?'

'I believe so,' George said distantly. He had no wish to
enter into conversation about his friends.

'Dreadful thing, those bodies being left outside the house,'
Mrs Davidson said in her quick, nervous voice. 'In a place
like North Park, too. It makes you wonder if anywhere's
safe these days.'

'And mark my words, they'll never find those responsible,'
Davidson opined. 'The first few days are crucial in a murder
case; once the trail's gone cold, the police might as well
throw their hand in.'

'Oh, surely not, Phil,' his wife protested. 'You often hear
of people being caught years later.'

'Only if they're in prison for something else, and bragging
to their cellmates. You'll see: it'll stop being newsworthy in
another week or so, and everyone'll forget it.'

'I doubt if the police will,' George commented. 'They're
probably pulling all the stops out, even if it's not reported
in the press.'

'Gang warfare, if you ask me; known football hooligans,
getting what was coming to them.'

'Really, dear, I don't think that's quite fair. They—'

George's attention strayed and he glanced again in
Jeremy's direction. The discussion was still going on, with

one of the men doing a fair amount of hand-waving. That a deal was in progress was certain, but George was unsure who was buying and who selling.

At their own table, Mr Davidson was signalling for the bill, and as, minutes later, they walked towards the door, George excused himself for a moment and made a detour to Jeremy's table. None of the men noticed his approach.

'Good evening,' he said pleasantly. 'Enjoying your meal?'

Jeremy spun round, his hand knocking over his glass, which was fortunately empty. 'Oh—George,' he said weakly.

George waited, smiling, for the introductions which would surely follow. They were not forthcoming. Instead, Jeremy muttered something vague about business colleagues and the men across the table smiled and nodded. There was nothing for it but to smile and nod back and rejoin the Davidsons who were awaiting him by the door.

It would be interesting, George reflected, to see if Jeremy referred to the incident when they met the next evening at the Private View.

At The Gables, too, there had been an unexpected meeting. A middle-aged French couple who were being shown to a table further down the restaurant caught sight of the Clériots, and descended on them with much exclaiming and shaking of hands.

They were introduced as Monsieur and Madame Beynaud, near neighbours from Saumur.

'Incredible that we should meet this way!' gushed Madame. 'We had no idea you were visiting England. Since Madame your wife is not with you, I presume it is a business trip? Ourselves, we are on holiday. A charming region, is it not?'

It was several minutes before they remembered the maître d', patiently waiting to show them to their table, and, amid a deluge of expressions of mutual goodwill, allowed themselves to be led away and the Teal party resumed their meal.

And now it was drawing to an end and they were sitting over coffee, petits-fours and brandy. Monica, having declined coffee, sat contentedly half-listening to the conversation and idly tracing the pattern on her plate. Its distinctive style and colouring proclaimed it instantly as Broadshire Porcelain, as was all the china at The Gables. Mr Pendrick believed in supporting home industry and doubtless the firm received many export orders as a result of his loyalty.

Pendrick was in the hall as they left, and as he shook her hand, Monica remembered Webb's message. 'Chief Inspector Webb asked to be remembered to you,' she told him, and felt the jerk of his hand in hers. Startled, she looked up, catching a fleeting expression which she couldn't analyse. Then he smiled a little grimly and said, 'Nice of him. We crossed swords a few years back.' He paused. 'I hope yours was a social meeting?'

'Unfortunately, no. It was in connection with the White murders.'

'Of course—how clumsy of me. I'm so sorry.'

She smiled and moved towards the door that Justin was holding open for her. But as she settled herself in the car, she could see Pendrick through the glass door of the hotel still looking after her. It was the last time she'd pass on a message from a policeman! she thought feelingly.

Eloise Teal would have been surprised, even startled, to know how much the members of her catering team knew of her personal affairs. It was not that the young people were overly curious, merely that, doing the local circuit in a dozen or so homes, they were more or less bound to pick up titbits of information.

Occasionally they witnessed surreptitiously linked hands beneath the table, the swift passage of a note, expertly palmed, a hurried drawing apart as they entered a room. But although they exchanged the odd ribaldry with each other, they were unfailingly discreet.

The girl, Diane, was the sister of one young man and the

girlfriend of the other. Business was thriving as news of their expertise spread, and the Tuesday morning found them rapidly preparing the canapés for the Private View before dashing out to serve lunch for six at Chedbury.

'Give me a dinner-party any day,' Graham grumbled. 'All these little bits and pieces are so time-consuming. What was the final figure—a round two hundred?'

'That's right,' his sister confirmed. 'Mr Reid said we can have the offices at the back to serve from. They're interconnected and I don't think there's much room, so we'll need all the stacking trays we can find.'

'He said they'll open the doors to the courtyard if it stays dry. It'd help if people moved outside to eat, but since there's nothing to look at out there, they might not.'

'Bet Mrs Teal won't throw one of her "migraines" this evening,' Diane remarked with a smile. 'She never does, when there's anything interesting. Mind over matter, they call it.'

'Or something!' Nick grinned. 'Just as well we're the Three Wise Monkeys—See All, Hear All, Say Nowt!'

'Too true,' Graham agreed. 'If they realized how much we knew, we'd have to sign the Official Secrets Act.'

Diane's thoughts had moved on. 'They've got some lovely things in that gallery,' she said guilelessly, looking up from the prawns in aspic. 'And it's my birthday soon.'

The young men snorted in unison. 'Nothing doing there, hon. The way those prices go, you'll have to wait till we're doing snacks at Buck House!'

At 11.30 that morning, George received an urgent phone call at the bank. His mother had collapsed and been rushed to the General Hospital.

It took him less than five minutes to terminate the interview he was giving and pass the rest of his morning appointments to his deputy. Then he set off on foot for the hospital. Mid-morning Shillingham was so congested with traffic that he reasoned it would be quicker to walk than try to manœuvre his car through the clogged streets.

Sunday's threatened thunder had not materialized and now the sun was back, reflected glaringly in shop windows and beating down on his head as he hurried along.

He shouldn't have left her last night, he thought in an agony of remorse. She'd said she didn't feel well. But then she always said that when he went out, and he'd learned to harden his heart. She wouldn't like being sent to the General, either; many was the promise she'd extracted from him that 'if anything happened' she'd be taken to Birch Lawn, the private nursing home.

Franklyn Road was jammed with people strolling along, pausing to chat, blocking the pavement outside the Arts Centre to read the notices of forthcoming events. Was he the only man in the world in a hurry?

He stepped off the pavement to avoid an animated group, and received a warning honk from an indignant motorist. Then, at last, he reached the corner of Carrington Street and turned thankfully into it.

His mother, he learned from the desk in the entrance, was in Intensive Care, but she was asking for him. Perspiring freely by now, he went up in the lift and was escorted to her bedside. She looked ghastly, he thought, his alarm deepening. A series of tubes linked her with ominous-looking machines and she was wearing an oxygen mask. He sat down on the chair beside the bed and took her hand in both his.

'It's all right, Mother, I'm here. Everything's going to be fine. Don't try to speak!' he added hastily, as she appeared to be struggling for words. 'Just lie still and regain your strength.'

'She keeps asking to be taken to Birch Lawn,' the nurse murmured in his ear, 'but of course she can't be moved. In any case, they haven't the facilities that we have. That's why the ambulance brought her straight here.' She moved away, and George rose and followed her.

'How serious is it?' he whispered. There was a fair amount of noise in the ward, and he was confident they couldn't be overheard.

'A minor attack, but serious enough at her age. She'll need a lot of rest.'

It was on the tip of his tongue to say that all she ever did was rest, but it seemed inappropriate. 'She's not in any immediate danger?'

'Not unless she has a relapse. The first twenty-four hours are crucial.'

'What brought it on, does anyone know?'

'Your housekeeper could tell you more, but I think she found her slumped in the chair when she took in her elevenses.'

Betsy; poor old Betsy, who always got the rough end of the stick and never any thanks for it.

'Just five minutes, Mr Latimer. Then I think you should go, and let her get some rest. You can see her again this evening.'

This evening; so much for the Private View, he thought, and was immediately ashamed that he could consider it at such a time. But he wouldn't after all be able to tax Jeremy about his anonymous companions.

The next five minutes were not easy, and he spent them trying to reassure his mother, grateful for the imposed time limit; a fact which caused him further guilt.

Having duly left her, he returned to the bank, walking slowly this time and allowing himself to be buffeted by people who were now, perversely, in more of a hurry than he was. Back at his desk he phoned first Betsy, who could tell him little more than he knew, and then Monica.

'Oh George, I'm so sorry!' she exclaimed. 'How is she now?'

He repeated the guarded information the nurse had given him. 'But I'm afraid I shan't be able to call for you this evening.'

'Goodness, as if that matters!' Monica paused. 'I hope you're not blaming yourself in any way?'

'I went out to dinner last night, though she asked me not to.'

'She *always* asks you not to! If she had her way, you'd never leave the house!' Another pause, then: 'Sorry!'

'You're right, of course. But we don't know how long she'd been lying in her chair before Betsy found her. If it had happened when I was home, it might have been different.'

'She's as tough as old boots. She'll pull through.'

George nodded, though Monica couldn't see him. Added to his sense of guilt was the fact that he'd been wondering lately whether to call his mother's bluff and go ahead with the wedding. It couldn't really be possible, he'd reasoned, to have a heart attack to order. After this, though, their plans would have to be shelved again. Perhaps she really was as ill as she kept telling everyone.

'Would you like me to come to the hospital with you?' Monica was asking.

'No, really. She's in Intensive Care and I'm the only one who can see her.'

'It would be moral support on the way there.'

He felt a rush of love for her. 'Bless you, darling,' he said quietly, 'but no. You go to the Private View; you've had a bad week yourself and could do with some light relief. I'll phone you later and let you know how she is.'

And, turning from the phone, he tried to pick up the threads of his traumatically interrupted day.

The Preston boy worked at the Job Centre in Duke Street, and Dawson and Cummings were waiting for him when he came out for lunch. He nodded as they introduced themselves.

'I reckoned you'd be looking me up, after seeing Dolores. And Mum said if you did, to ask when the funeral is?'

Dawson was taken aback. 'It's not been arranged yet, son. We have to wait till we can charge someone with the crime.'

'But that could be years!' Damien protested, unconsciously echoing Phil Davidson.

Dawson ignored the slur on his professional competence.

'Weeks, perhaps,' he corrected, 'but the Coroner has the last word on that one. I'll make a note to let you know when it's fixed.'

'Ta.'

'Got a set lunch-hour, have you?'

'Till half-one, yeah.'

'Like to turn in here, then?' They were passing a McDonald's.

'Don't mind.'

The unlikely trio went through the doors together, Dawson and the boy seating themselves while Cummings ordered beefburgers and Coke. Not the skipper's usual tipple, he thought with a grin.

The lad was subdued, obviously grieving for his friends as much as his sister did.

'I believe you last saw the Whites four weeks ago?'

'That's right, we went to the Indian for a meal.'

'Did they mention any particular aggro, anyone who might have it in for them?'

'Don't think so, but they was always scrapping with someone. No hard feelings, though, once it was over.' Damien munched solidly on his beefburger.

Dawson went through the usual questions, though merely as a matter of form. Preston seemed pathetically eager to help, and if he knew anything, he'd have told them.

'Akcherly,' Damien said suddenly, 'I've just thought—I did see Rob after that, but only for a minute, like. He was setting up his ladder outside the chip shop.'

Both detectives instinctively leaned forward. 'You spoke to him?'

The boy seemed taken aback. 'Yeh, but it was nothing important, like. He was asking about aeroplanes.'

'*Aeroplanes?*'

'Yeh, well, they're a hobby of mine, see. I've got model kits and pictures of them all round my room.'

Dawson found he'd been holding his breath. 'Hang on a minute, lad. When was this?

'A week or two back.'

'Look, Damien, this could be important. Think hard.'

The boy looked frightened. 'It must have been a Wednesday, because I'd been to the post office.'

'Which Wednesday?'

His face cleared. 'The week before last. I remember now —I'd just bought a card for Dolores. It was her birthday next day, and Rob gave me a fiver to get something.'

Four days after the house had been done and the low-flying aircraft reported.

'What did he want to know about planes?' Dawson asked quietly.

'The makes of the smaller ones, mainly. How far they could fly, if they'd need extra fuel to get to the continent— that kind of thing.'

'And what did you tell him?'

'Well, the one he described sounded like a Cessna.'

'He described one? Why?'

'I dunno. I did ask, but he was cagey, like. Said he'd seen a picture of it. And I hadn't time to stop, because I was due back.'

'Can you remember anything else he said?'

Damien stopped chewing and frowned, concentrating. After a minute, he shook his head. 'No, I reckon that was all.'

Nevertheless, it was a great deal more than they'd expected. There seemed little doubt now that the twins *had* seen the plane land and stopped to investigate. And that their curiosity, like that of the cat, had led to their death.

CHAPTER 11

During the drive to Broadminster, Claudia's mind had been circling round and round the state of her marriage. The crisis had developed so suddenly that she could still hardly believe it; it was almost as if Abbie's innocent remark over lunch that day had precipitated disaster—though if her present suspicions were correct, her marriage had never been the happy, trusting relationship she'd imagined.

For she was now as sure as she could be that Harry and Eloise were having an affair—if a relationship which had presumably lasted twenty years could be so described. The vaguely unsettled feeling of the last week had crystallized last evening when, ashamed of her stilted behaviour on Sunday, she had phoned Eloise to apologize.

Her apprehension about phoning was on more than one count; she'd seen Monica that afternoon, who, when Claudia inquired after her headache, had told her Eloise was now suffering from one and she was standing in for her at a business dinner that evening.

However, anxious to clear the air before the View, Claudia went ahead with her call, intending to tell whoever answered not to disturb Eloise if she were resting.

She was considerably surprised to learn that in fact she had gone out. Then, with a terrible understanding, she remembered the phone call which Harry had taken during dinner, and his hasty departure after the meal 'to attend to a crisis at the Gallery'.

She had made some stupid, incoherent reply to Theo, who was still waiting for her message, and put the phone down. Almost she was tempted to go straight down to the Gallery on the pretext of offering help. But she didn't dare. Suppose she did find them together, what could she say? She was no good at scenes, inclined to burst into tears rather than stand her ground and give as good as she got. And suppose, after all this time, it would be a relief for them to end the deceit? Was she prepared to let Harry go? What of Abbie? And Justin and the boys? Had she the right to precipitate the disruption of so many lives?

On the other hand, perhaps Justin already knew? Yet he gave no hint of it, always so pleasant and welcoming whenever they saw him. He had probably been duped as much as she had.

By the time Claudia reached Broadminster her mind was no clearer than when she left home, and she continued to debate the problem while automatically negotiating the familiar streets. She had been born in the town and lived there until, when she was nineteen, the family moved to Shillingham and she had met Harry: Harry who, two years previously, had been jilted by Eloise Tovey.

It was as well, she thought as she turned into her friend's drive, that she had this lunch engagement today; hanging about at home with her worries would have been insupportable. She remembered Eloise's casual offer to help with the hanging, and smiled grimly to herself. Once this evening was over, she'd decide what to do.

A passing car recalled her to her surroundings, and she realized she was still sitting in the driveway clutching the steering-wheel. Hastily she released it and, gathering up her handbag and the potted plant she'd brought as a gift, she got out of the car.

Tony Reid, manager of the Carlton Gallery, was distinctly on edge. He was the one who held the can on such occasions, and if anything went wrong, the blame would be laid squarely at his door.

In his early thirties, he was a presentable young man with a slightly artistic air that went down well with customers. He was also very ambitious, which appealed to Harry. He'd set his heart on owning his own gallery, and every penny he earned was salted away to that end. He was unmarried, but whether his interests lay in other directions, Harry neither knew nor cared. With his acute brain, his deferential manner, and his willingness to stick his neck out when necessary, he was ideal for the job.

During the morning they had worked methodically hanging the paintings and sketches. Having performed the task many times together, they worked well as a team and had almost completed it. Now, in the lunch hour, they'd gone across the road to the wine bar.

'Relax, Tony,' Harry advised, noting the younger man's tension. 'We've done all we can; it's in the lap of the gods now.'

'Trouble is, the gods are a fickle bunch, and quite likely to throw mud in your eye for no good reason.'

'Wine all organized?' Justin's firm was supplying it, as always on these occasions.

'Yes, they're delivering it at five, so the white will stay cool as long as possible.'

'And the caterers? No problem there?' It was the first time they'd used Home Cooking, having previously relied on a couple of girls from the wine bar they were now patronizing.

'I phoned to confirm, and got the bloody answering machine. Probably means they've fitted in another job before us.'

'Well, we haven't exclusive claim on them. They're dependable, though; I've been to several dinner-parties they've masterminded, and they were superb.'

Probably at Mrs Teal's, Tony thought morosely. He resented the way she made herself so much at home at the Gallery simply because she belonged to the same Arts Society as the Marlows. If that *was* the reason, he reflected darkly. Not like Mrs Marlow, who never interfered but was always pleasant and polite. Nice lady, Mrs Marlow.

'I told them they could use the offices,' he said. 'That'll be all right, won't it?'

'Yes, I'll clear my desk when we get back. How about upstairs? I've not been up this morning.'

'All in place. It looks very impressive.'

'Good. Well, drink up. We'd better get back and finish the final check. After that, all we can do is say our prayers and hope it goes off all right. And,' he added with a smile, fishing out his credit card, 'that your fickle gods aren't in the mood for mud slinging.'

'Hannah?'

'Hello, David. How's the case going?'

'Chugging along. A few facts are slotting into place, but nothing of significance.'

'Did the van-driver show up?'

'Yes, and he seems to be in the clear. Which means we now haven't even got a suspect. Look, it's five-thirty and my brain's ground to a halt. I think I'll take an evening off and come back to it fresh tomorrow. Are you free? I thought we could eat somewhere cheap and cheerful and perhaps take in a film.'

'Oh, David, I'm sorry, I can't. I'm going to the Carlton Gallery with Gwen and Dilys. Monica wangled us invitations.'

'Just my luck. Well, have a good time with all those VIPs. Incidentally—' his voice quickened—'the Gallery was on the Whites' window-cleaning list. It wouldn't hurt to keep your eyes and ears open.'

'With two hundred-odd people milling about? Even if they were up to something, it'd be under wraps this evening.'

'You're probably right.'

'I'm sorry I can't join you; in this weather, I don't relish the prospect of masses of people in a confined space.'

'What you mean is, you'd rather spend the evening in my scintillating company.'

'Exactly!'

'Enjoy yourself,' he said, and rang off.

Poor David, Hannah thought; he'd probably have enjoyed the View more than she would. Modern art was not really her scene.

Since Harry wanted to be back at the Gallery by six o'clock, it was arranged that the Teals should call for Claudia and Abbie.

Hearing the car arrive, Claudia went to the door in time to see Justin opening the back and lifting a case of wine out of the boot.

'This is for Harry with my compliments,' he said as he carried it up the path. 'It's the Chablis he particularly enjoyed last week.'

'Oh, Justin, that is kind of you.' Her voice shook, and he glanced at her in surprise.

'It's no big deal. He's a good customer, and this is just a way of saying thank you.'

There was a lump in Claudia's throat as she watched him lay the box down in the hallway. Just how grateful would he be to Harry by the end of the week, if she carried out her intentions?

And now she had to face Eloise: who was, as usual, looking striking, her flaxen hair like a curtain of silk, her large spectacles complimenting rather than detracting from her appearance. Claudia, climbing into the back of the car with Abbie, said lightly, 'Head better?'

'Clear as a bell, thank you.'

'Did Theo receive his invitation?' she asked, for Abbie's benefit.

'Yes, he's going along with Jeremy and Primrose.'

There was a continental air about Shillingham that evening. Bar customers were standing outside, glasses in hand, and where space permitted, chairs and tables had been set up on the pavements. Girls in thin, pretty dresses strolled along chatting to their shirt-sleeved companions, and sun blinds were in evidence on several buildings.

'If this is the greenhouse effect, I'm all for it!' Abbie remarked.

'You wouldn't be if you had to water the garden every evening,' Justin rejoined. He parked in his own firm's car park, which was only a few hundred yards from the Gallery, and as they turned the corner into Carlton Road they were met by the swelling hum of many voices.

'Sounds as if it's already in full swing,' Justin said.

When they reached the Gallery, the noise which greeted them was overwhelming. Well-dressed people holding wine glasses were thronging the room and the atmosphere was stifling, despite the open door at the far end which gave on to the courtyard. Almost immediately they caught sight of Monica and her mother, standing in front of a striking painting of a Provençal village.

Justin said in Monica's ear, 'I took it upon myself to ask the Clériots to look in. They're not flying back till tomorrow and were at a loose end. I'm sure Harry won't mind. Let me know if you catch sight of them.' He looked about him. 'George not with you?'

'No, his mother collapsed this morning. She's in the General, in Intensive Care.'

'Oh dear,' Justin said, and Monica knew he was wondering how she'd feel if the old lady were to die. She was wondering herself; as long as Mrs Latimer was alive, she herself was under no pressure to marry George, but it was tacitly assumed their wedding would take place soon after her death. Certainly any grief on her part would be short-lived; the old lady had been consistently rude and un-pleasant to her, and bullied poor George mercilessly. Her main concern was for George himself, who had been such a devoted son. She hoped very much that he wouldn't expect his wife to take over the rôle of matriarch.

Abbie, meanwhile, had caught sight of Theo with his brother and Primrose, and made her way over to them. Theo looked very dashing, she thought, in a blue linen jacket and fawn trousers.

'Hello, Abbie. Exams looming?'

She pulled a face. 'Don't remind me! I've just seen Miss James and Miss Rutherford, and I should be at home revising. But it's too hot to study, it stews your brains.'

'In my opinion, exams are a waste of time,' Primrose said in a bored voice. 'They don't prepare you for real life, do they?'

'Depends what you consider real life, my sweet,' Jeremy replied.

Though Abbie agreed with Primrose, she played devil's advocate. 'It also depends what you want to do; I—' She broke off. A middle-aged man was approaching them, lead-ing by the hand the girl Theo had met in the park. Oh *sugar*! she thought. Just when things were going so well!

The couple reached them and the man said breezily, 'Sorry to butt in; Theo, I'd like you to meet Christine Chase. She works for Darley Smythe, but we're on neutral ground here.'

Abbie waited for Theo to say they knew each other, but to her surprise he and the girl were shaking hands as though they'd never met.

'Always delighted to meet the opposition!' Theo said with his charming smile. 'How do you do? Can I get you a refill?' And, putting a hand under the girl's elbow, he steered her away.

'Smooth operator, my brother!' Jeremy remarked, almost by way of apology. 'What about you, Abbie? What are you drinking?'

'White wine, please.' What were they playing at? she wondered. If she could get Theo alone, she'd jolly well ask him.

Monica, glancing towards the door, noticed the Clériots standing there, and as she couldn't immediately see Justin, made her way over to them.

There was a double entrance to the Gallery, the door that opened off the street giving on to a short passage which ended in a flight of stairs leading to the room above. The Gallery itself was approached through a glass door immediately on the left, and it was here that the two Frenchmen were standing. They greeted her with relief, overwhelmed by so much English being spoken at such volume. In order to make herself heard, Monica gestured them back into the passage, where a welcome breath of air was coming through the open street door.

'And they say the English climate is cold and wet!' the senior Clériot marvelled, mopping his brow.

'We have our moments! Once you've recovered your breath we'll go in search of some wine. There are some very interesting paintings; I think you'll enjoy looking at them.'

They continued chatting in French, and after a moment or two Monica became aware that someone was hovering behind her. She turned to see Harry's manager, Tony Reid.

'Excuse me, madam, may I have a word with these gentlemen?'

She smiled and nodded, then realized with a jolt of

surprise that he was waiting for her to leave them. Hiding her embarrassment, she said to the Clériots, 'I'll bring you some wine,' and pushed her way back into the Gallery. What extraordinary behaviour! She'd have a word with Harry about that young man. In any case, whatever could he have to say to the Frenchmen that she might not hear? Perhaps, she thought suddenly, he'd discovered they weren't on the invitation list? But surely he wouldn't be so ungracious as to ask them to leave?

Prepared to argue their case, she manœuvred her way back to the door, but as she reached it they reappeared, looking bewildered.

'That was most bizarre,' the younger one told her. 'It seemed he wished us to go upstairs—I do not know for what reason.'

'How peculiar. Did you go?'

'We started to, but then another gentleman approached and said there had been an error.' And he shrugged eloquently at the ways of the English.

Monica was equally puzzled, but by this time Justin had caught sight of them, and was approaching with glasses of wine. Leaving the Clériots in his care, she went in search of her mother.

At eight o'clock the catering team started serving refreshments, stressing that food and wine were available in the courtyard. People obediently drifted out there, and, able to move more freely, Monica took the chance to study the paintings. A partition had been erected, forming two walkways, and as she moved along she could hear murmured comments from the other side of the screen. Then her attention was caught by a woman speaking softly but volubly in French. Curious, she quickened her step and, coming to the end of the aisle, rounded the partition and looked down the adjacent one. It was the couple who had spoken to them at The Gables. The Entente Cordiale was certainly being observed, she thought, and wondered if they, too, were uninvited guests. Not wanting to become involved in conversation with them, she returned to her own aisle and her perusal of the paintings.

Abbie spotted Theo at the far end of the courtyard, filling a plate with a selection of canapés. She went purposefully towards him.

'Why did you pretend not to know that girl?' she asked bluntly.

He turned, a startled look on his face, but asked lightly, 'What girl? What are you talking about, young Abbie?'

'Christine Chase, or whatever her name was.'

'But I didn't know her,' Theo protested, popping a twist of smoked salmon into her mouth. 'Whatever made you think I did?'

'Because I saw you with her in the park,' Abbie said through the smoked salmon.

Theo looked at he consideringly. 'Did you, indeed?'

'Well?' she prompted.

'All right. Look, there are reasons, but I can't go into them here.' He hesitated. 'Are you going to school tomorrow?'

'Just in the morning.'

'Suppose we have lunch then, and I'll explain?'

Abbie stared at him, a tide of colour flooding her face. Lunch with Theo—it hardly seemed possible.

'Is that OK?'

She nodded, not trusting her voice.

'Good girl. And in the meantime, I'm sure I can depend on you not to say anything. You'll understand why when I explain.' He patted her arm. 'The fair Primrose is waiting for sustenance—I must go. Twelve-thirty at the Maypole?'

She nodded. 'Right. Thanks,' and stood looking after him as he disappeared into the throng. Thank goodness she hadn't stayed at home with her history books, she thought fervently.

'Tulie darling, how good to see you!' Eloise slid an arm round the narrow, black-encased shoulders and planted a swift kiss on the highly rouged cheek.

'Good evening, Mrs Teal.'

'Have you had something to eat?'

'No, I haven't fought my way to the refreshments yet.'

'Jeremy'll get you something.' Eloise signalled to her elder son half-way down the room, and in dumb show made her request known. He nodded and set off for the court-yard.

Miss Tulip said approvingly, 'I'm glad you chose the lilac for this evening. It's most becoming.'

'Thank you; I'm very pleased with it.' Miss Tulip had played a large part in moulding Eloise's dress sense, and she remained deeply grateful. 'I hear you've had quite an exciting time lately, with visits from the police?'

Miss Tulip shot her an apprehensive look. 'It was Miss Monica they came to see.'

'I know, but upsetting for you just the same.' Perhaps, Eloise was thinking, that accounted for Tulie's rather strained expression. 'Apart from that, is all going well?'

Miss Tulip paused before replying. Was Miss Eloise, as she still privately thought of her, merely making conver-sation, or was she fishing? And if so, what had put her on the track? Perhaps the policemen's visits had something to do with her after all.

'Tulie? Is something wrong?'

Miss Tulip took a wisp of lace handkerchief out of her black clutch bag and patted her mouth. 'No, my dear, nothing other than the heat.'

'Yes, it is overpowering. Would you like to sit down?'

'I spend my life standing, Mrs Teal, as you know. I'm perfectly all right.'

Jeremy was shouldering his way back with a plate piled high with titbits and a glass of wine. Miss Tulip's eyes softened. They'd been such lovely little boys, he and his brother. Many was the time she'd pushed their pram round the town while their mother tried on dresses. He stooped to give her a kiss and she felt herself relax. She was being over-sensitive—there'd been nothing hidden in Mrs Teal's remarks. But the sooner this police business was cleared up, the easier she'd be. Delicately, like a robin at a bird-table, she began to eat.

Hannah was uncomfortably sticky and her new shoes were pinching her feet. She glanced at Gwen, who also looked hot and bothered, spraying hairpins with every movement as strands of hair detached themselves from her French pleat.

'How about slipping away and relaxing somewhere with a salad and a long cold drink?'

'Sounds wonderful, if you don't think Monica would mind.'

'She might even join us; I'm sure Dilys will.'

Monica when approached accepted with alacrity. She was finding the Clériots heavy going and George was increasingly on her mind. She was anxious to phone him to inquire after his mother.

Eloise being quite agreeable to dropping off her mother on the way home, the four friends thankfully escaped from the mêlée and strolled across the road to the wine bar. It too had a courtyard behind it, filled now with people sitting under brightly coloured umbrellas.

While the others found a table, Monica went to make her phone call. But it was Betsy who answered; George was still at the hospital and there was no further news. Monica left an appropriate message, said she'd ring again in the morning, and went out to join the others.

Their orders taken and their drinks served, they settled down to talk over the evening.

'Buy anything, anybody?' Gwen inquired.

'I've reserved a couple of prints,' Monica said. 'I'll pop in and have another look at them tomorrow.'

'I wonder what was going on upstairs?' Dilys mused, as the waiter set their salads on the table.

'How do you mean?'

'Well, I went out into the passage for a breath of air and was pretty smartly escorted back again.'

'Who by?' Hannah asked, mindful of Webb's instructions.

'One of the officials, I suppose—a young man with long-ish hair. He was very apologetic and said they had to keep the exit clear, but I could hear voices up above and it sounded as if someone was about to come downstairs. So, being of a curious turn of mind, I hung around near the door, and sure enough a couple appeared from that direction and came into the Gallery. They were talking French.'

Monica frowned. 'Two men?'

'No, a man and a woman.'

'That's odd,' she said, and related the episode with Tony Reid and the Clériots.

'An illicit game of roulette, no doubt,' suggested Dilys, and there, having no better explanation, they let the matter rest.

When Hannah arrived back at Beechcroft Mansions an hour or so later, she took the lift beyond her own floor and knocked on Webb's front door. He opened it in shirt-sleeves.

'Ah, the reveller's return! How did it go?'

'Interesting. Can you spare a few minutes?'

'Do you have to ask?'

She walked through to his living-room. A lamp was lit in one corner, but most of the room was in shadow. Mozart was playing softly on the stereo and Webb's old leather chair had been pulled over to the wide-open window.

'I was trying to get some air. Drink?'

'I'd love a gin and tonic. I've been on wine all evening.'

He pulled a chair over for her and she sat down, relaxing into its sagging embrace.

'Well,' she began, accepting the glass he handed her, 'I kept my ears and eyes open as instructed.'

'And?'

'And there was something rather puzzling.' She repeated what both Dilys and Monica had told her about the appar-ently out-of-bounds area upstairs. 'The strange thing was that both couples involved were French.'

Webb smiled, thinking of Jackson's comment about sinister foreigners. Perhaps he'd been nearer the mark than either of them realized.

'You think the first couple was mistaken for the second?'

'It rather looks like that.'

Webb tipped his glass, letting the ice clink against the sides. 'Any idea what they could have been up to?'

'Not the remotest.'

'Or if anyone else went up?'

'No.'

He said reflectively, 'I know the manager, I've chatted to him once or twice. Not Marlow, though. Have you met him?'

'No, but Monica sometimes speaks of him.' She paused. 'Are you wondering what the Whites saw through those upstairs windows?'

'I certainly wouldn't mind a look up there. Well done, love, you've opened another line of inquiry, and at this stage of the game it's more than welcome.'

At three minutes to twelve that night, Ethel Latimer finally released her hold on life and slipped peacefully away.

CHAPTER 12

Monica heard the news the next morning; George phoned as she was preparing to leave for work.

'Oh my dear, I'm so sorry!' she exclaimed. 'Were you with her?'

'Yes; it was very peaceful. I think they knew by the time I arrived that she wasn't going to pull through.'

'I should have been there,' Monica said remorsefully. 'Is there anything I can do?'

'No, thank you. Everything's very straightforward.' It would be; George was nothing if not methodical.

'May I come round this evening?'

There was a slight pause. Then he said, 'If you'd like to, I'd be glad to see you.'

The time arranged, Monica replaced the phone thoughtfully. The news had come as a surprise; although illogically in the circumstances, she hadn't expected Mrs Latimer to die. Now, for the first time, she would meet George without the ever-present shadow of his mother. Unless, that is, her influence persisted.

At the Marlow home breakfast had been subdued, though Abbie, hugging her secret to herself, did not appear to notice. 'I'll be home about two-thirty,' she said with studied carelessness as she left for school.

Claudia looked up dully. 'I was expecting you for lunch.'

'Not today. See you later.' And she was gone. As the front door slammed behind her, Claudia, without previous thought, heard herself say, 'How long has Eloise been your mistress?'

She saw the shock on Harry's face but it brought no satisfaction.

'Claudia! Is that what you think?'

'It's what I know.'

'But that's ludicrous! Whatever—'

'You met on Monday evening—you can't deny it.'

Staring at her, he made no attempt to. She slammed her hand on the table. 'If I hadn't been such a fool, I'd have realized years ago. I suppose it's been going on all our married life?'

He was still staring helplessly at her, his face white, and she burst out, 'Haven't you *ever* loved me?'

That galvanized him and he reached across the table, seizing both her hands. 'Darling, I've *always* loved you! I still do.'

'You've an odd way of showing it,' she said, pulling her hands free. 'Does Justin know?'

'Know what?' he blustered, but his eyes fell under her accusing gaze.

'Let's stop playing games, Harry. I should have realized Eloise would still consider you her property. But she's always been so *friendly*. How could she *do* it?' She put her head in her hands.

After a long, pulsing silence, Harry said, 'She's fond of you. We never intended to hurt either you or Justin.'

'It's simply that we don't fulfil your needs? Oh well, fair enough.' The bitterness in her voice cut into him.

'Darling, please don't talk like that. What we've done is wrong—God, I know that—but if it had ever occurred to me you'd find out, I'd never have gone on with it, I swear it.'

'It was all right as long as I didn't know?'

He said miserably, 'That's not what I meant. I can't expect you to understand, but Eloise got into my blood a long time ago. I was never really sure of her, though. I think she only agreed to marry me because it was romantic to be engaged while she was still at school.'

'And then she met Justin,' Claudia said flatly.

'Yes.'

Twisting the knife, she added, 'Well, go on. When did it start up again?'

His eyes fell. 'When I met you. She was jealous, and I, fool that I was, was flattered. I thought I'd lost her, and it suddenly seemed that I hadn't.'

'I'm surprised you bothered to marry me, then.'

'Claudia, I fell in love with you, and I've never stopped loving you. You must believe that.'

'And no doubt she's equally devoted to Justin.' It seemed incredible they were having this conversation, and suddenly she'd had enough of it. 'You'd better go,' she said, 'it's time to open the Gallery.'

'But I can't just leave you. I want you to—'

'Please go, Harry. You've said enough.'

He stood up reluctantly, looking down at her bent head. 'What are you going to do?'

'I haven't decided.'

'Abbie—'

'Yes, Abbie!' she broke in furiously. 'You never considered her in all this, but no doubt you'll expect me to.'

He lifted his hand and let it fall. Then he turned and left the room. Claudia went on sitting there for several minutes. Then, drawing a deep breath, she stood up and started to clear the table.

It was not Harry's day; he arrived at the Gallery to find Webb and Jackson already waiting for him. He'd seen the taller man here before, talking to Tony quite knowledgeably about the paintings, and did not at first realize they were detectives.

'Yes, gentlemen; can I help you?'

The warrant card was produced and he felt in his stomach the cold sensation that even innocent people experience in such circumstances.

'I hope so, Mr Marlow,' Webb said pleasantly. He glanced at the long screens dividing the length of the Gallery, and the paintings hung on both sides of them. 'An exhibition on, I see.'

'That's right; why don't you take a look round?'

'I believe you held a Private View last night?'

'Yes, an excellent turn-out. As you can see, a lot of the paintings are already sold.'

Webb fingered one of the catalogues lying on the counter. 'What was on display upstairs?' he asked casually, and looked up in time to catch the younger man's involuntary movement.

There was the briefest of pauses, then Marlow said, 'There was nothing on display upstairs. It's storage space, not open to the public.'

'But I believe several people were shown up there?'

'Ah, you mean the framers. They'd some business to discuss and as we couldn't make ourselves heard downstairs, we went up for a few minutes.'

French framers? Webb said impassively, 'All right if we have a look?'

'Well, it's probably in a mess, packing cases and so on.'

'Actually it's quite tidy, Mr Marlow.' Tony Reid had come forward. 'I sorted it out a bit when I got in.'

Marlow shrugged. 'Very well.' He led the way into the passage and up the steep staircase, Webb and Jackson at his heels. At the top of the stairs a small window faced them, presumably looking out over the back courtyard. On their right was a door marked 'WC' and on their left another led to the large storage area above the Gallery.

Webb looked about him with interest. The far end of it was, as Marlow had said, filled with sheets of cardboard, packing cases and stacks of paintings in frames, no doubt temporarily removed from below to house the exhibition. Several items of furniture were shrouded under dust sheets and a pair of steps leant against the wall.

At the near end, however, a fairly large space had been kept clear. There was a Victorian chaise-longue under the window, a couple of button-back chairs and a few occasional tables. Almost like a private sitting-room, in fact.

'Have your lunch up here, do you?' Webb asked facetiously. He looked at the window, screened by a Venetian blind. Had the White boys seen anything through it? It was hard to imagine what it could have been.

'How many people were here last night, Mr Marlow?'

'About two hundred. Too many, actually, in this weather.'

'I presume you have a guest list?'

'I have, yes. Look, Chief Inspector, do you mind telling me what this is all about?'

'Just a line of inquiry we're pursuing, sir. May we borrow the list?'

'Would it make any difference if I said no?'

'It's your privilege, sir,' Webb replied blandly.

'Mr Reid has it.' Marlow's voice was short. Apparently his patience with them had evaporated. Jackson, catching Webb's eye, pulled his mouth down as Marlow went ahead of them down the stairs. The list was duly produced and handed over.

'Had your windows cleaned lately?' Webb asked, as he flicked through it.

'You have an agile mind, Chief Inspector,' Marlow said drily. 'I confess I can't keep up with you. Why should you be interested in my windows?'

'I wondered if you'd managed to replace your previous cleaners.'

'And why should I do that?'

'For the very good reason that they're dead.'

Marlow stared at him with a complete lack of comprehension.

'Didn't you realize, sir? Those two lads who were murdered last week; they had a window-cleaning round in the town centre. You were one of their customers.'

'Good God!' Marlow said softly. 'So that's why you're here.'

'That's right. All the premises they serviced are being examined.'

'But—why, for God's sake?'

'It's possible they might have seen something during the course of their work which led to their deaths.'

'I see. Any idea what?'

'Not as yet, sir, no. We're working on it.'

'Well, good luck to you, but I'm afraid I can't help.'

The glass door beside them opened tentatively, and a girl put her head round. 'Excuse me, is the Gallery open?'

'Of course, madam, please come in. These gentlemen are just leaving.'

Which, Jackson reflected out on the pavement, was as smooth an ejection as they'd had for some time.

'What do you make of him, Guv?'

'I don't know. He wasn't keen for us to go upstairs, but it could have been for the reason he gave. Certainly he let us look our fill once we got there, so if anything untowards *had* been around last night, it must have been safely disposed of.'

'That bloke saying he'd tidied up might have reassured him.'

'Yes, I thought of that.' He looked across the road at the wine bar opposite. It was called The Vine Leaf, and its sign depicted a coy-looking Eve modestly shielding herself.

'Let's go and have a cool drink, Ken, and while we're there we can make inquiries about the couple over the road. No doubt they patronize the place.'

The man behind the bar, gratified to have such early customers, took their light ales out to the garden, where the policemen had seated themselves in the shade.

'I hear there was a big do last night across the road,' Webb began.

'That's right.'

'Involve you at all?'

He shook his head. 'They often borrow a couple of our girls to serve drinks, but this time they'd professional caterers.'

'You know the owner, then?'

'Mr Marlow? Yes, he usually comes over for lunch.'

So he didn't eat in his upstairs salon; perhaps he used it as a love-nest.

'Nice bloke?'

'One of the best.'

'And the other one?'

The barman grinned. 'Pleasant enough, but I keep my distance.'

Webb took a long drink. 'Mr Marlow's wife ever join him for lunch?' he asked, since the man still lingered by their table.

'Sometimes, and sometimes it's the other lady.' He stopped and coloured. 'Whoops! I probably shouldn't have said that!'

'What other lady would that be?' Webb asked innocently. Perhaps his flippant thought about love-nests had been on the button.

'Don't know who she is, but he calls her Louise or something. Smart piece, always well turned out.'

Webb gave him a conspiratorial wink. 'Reckon they're having it off?'

But the barman wouldn't be drawn. 'None of my business if they are.' Nor yours, mate, was the implication.

A woman and two young children had settled at another table, and the barman went across to take their orders.

'Any Louises on that list, Ken?'

'Not that I can see.'

'I think we'll have another word with Miss Tovey, she was there last night. Come to that, she might be able to fill us in on these French people.'

The old bird in the foyer at Randall Tovey nearly had a stroke when she saw them. Jackson was intrigued. What, he wondered, had she got to hide? She tottered towards them on spindly heels, her face chalk white beneath the painted red circles.

'Yes? What is it? You wish to see me?'

Webb, as startled as Jackson by this travesty, said politely, 'We'd like a word with Miss Tovey, please.'

Miss Tulip straightened her narrow shoulders and regarded him with a surprisingly steely gaze. 'I'd rather you said it to my face, if you don't mind,' she informed him.

Webb, keeping his own face blank, felt a shaft of excitement. She must know something, but how could this old crone have anything to do with the murders?

'You wish to make a statement, madam?'

She drew a deep breath. 'Yes, I think I do. I've had enough of this cat-and-mouse game.'

'Chief Inspector?' Miss Tovey's voice came from above them, and, turning, they saw her at the top of the stairs. Her eyes moved to the old woman, and she gave an exclamation. 'Tulie, what is it? Are you all right?'

'This lady has just indicated that she'd like to make a statement, Miss Tovey.'

'What on earth—?' Monica came running down the stairs. 'Tulie, are you ill? What's happened?'

'It's time it all came out, Miss Monica. I apologize for being such an inconvenience.'

'I haven't the faintest idea what you're talking about. These gentlemen are investigating a murder case.'

'That's what they say, I know, and I dare say that's part of it,' Miss Tulip conceded in a quavering voice. 'However, I'm fully aware that I'm under investigation, and I would much prefer them to come out and say so to my face, instead of troubling you about it.'

Monica took her arm, flashing an appealing look at Webb. 'I think we should all have a coffee and get this straightened out. I'm sure there's a simple explanation.'

She led the way to the tea-room, which was screened from the foyer behind ivy-twined columns. There was no one in there except a waitress setting out cups and saucers.

'Lucy, would you bring coffee for four and then leave us, please. And put the "Closed" notice in the entrance. I'll move it when we've finished.'

They seated themselves at a corner table at the far end, where no one could overhear their conversation. Webb had his usual difficulty fitting his legs into the confined space.

The coffee when it arrived was extremely good, and there was a plate of almond crisp biscuits which looked homemade. Jackson hoped they would sit easy on the light ale he'd just finished.

Webb cleared his throat. 'Miss—Tulip, is it? I don't know what you have to tell us, but perhaps I should caution you. That means that what you say will be taken down and if necessary may be used in evidence. Do you understand?'

'I expected nothing less,' she replied with dignity.

'Well, Tulie,' Monica said gently, 'what's it all about?'

It was to her that the old woman spoke, and Webb was content that it should be so. In fact, if she could forget his and Jackson's presence, so much the better. He noted approvingly that Jackson had his notebook on his knee, below the level of the table. No doubt the whole thing was a storm in a tea—or rather coffee—cup, he thought. But the story which emerged took them all by surprise.

Unlikely as it seemed, Miss Tulip was addicted to gambling, and had been for a considerable time. It had begun innocently enough with placing bets at the Broadminster races; yet within a few weeks the initial excitement had developed into a craving which could not be satisfied, and she became enmeshed with an illicit gambling syndicate.

'I knew it was wrong,' she admitted in her prim, high voice. 'I would wake in the night and vow I'd stop, but in my heart I knew I could not. You see, the excitement was like a fever. I can't begin to describe it, but it was not a pleasant feeling. I resented not being in control of myself, and I became more and more frightened that one day my luck would run out.

'The trouble was, you see, that I kept on winning. That was the extraordinary thing. So I told myself I was harming no one—in fact even doing some good, since I kept very little for myself. The money didn't interest me, it was the winning that counted.'

'What did you do with it?' Monica asked her.

The old lady made a dismissive gesture. 'It went to various charities—for children, mostly.' She leant forward anxiously. 'Miss Monica, I'm deeply ashamed. All I can say in mitigation is that it was my only vice. As you know, I've never smoked and I take only an occasional glass of wine.'

Monica Tovey was gazing at her with concern and sympathy, blaming herself for never, over the years, being aware of this self-inflicted anguish.

'I knew it couldn't last indefinitely,' Miss Tulip continued. 'I was breaking the law, and one day I should be punished for it.' She looked at Webb for the first time since she'd begun her story. 'Would you tell me, sir, how I gave myself away?'

He said gently, 'You didn't, ma'am.'

She gazed at him, her mouth working. 'You mean there was no need for me to make this statement?'

'No.'

She pursed her lips, considering. 'Nevertheless, I'm glad I have. It's been weighing on me more and more as time went on, and it's a relief to make a clean breast of it.' She turned to Monica, and her voice wavered only slightly as she said, 'I shall quite understand, my dear, if you'd prefer me to hand in my notice.'

Monica reached out and put her hand over the thin, freckled one plucking at the cloth. 'We couldn't manage without you, Tulie, you know that. There's no question of your going, unless you want to.' She looked at Webb. 'What happens now?'

'She'll probably be summonsed and prosecuted, but the fine will be only nominal. And if you'd consider giving evidence, ma'am, it'd be helpful. You were fortunate, but there are many who aren't and these illegal syndicates can be pretty ruthless. It's a chance to stamp this one out.'

They all looked at the old lady, who trembled slightly. 'I'll be guided by Miss Monica,' she said. 'As a magistrate, she'll be able to advise me. In the meantime, if you do not require me any longer, I must return to my desk.' She rose to her feet and they watched her thin, straight figure walk out of the tea-room.

'Well!' Monica said, leaning back in her chair. 'That was incredible. I'd no idea. Anyway, I'll deal with it later. In the meantime, what was it you really came to see me about?'

Webb wrested his mind back from the old lady. 'It concerns the Private View last night. I understand some French people were there?'

'Yes?'

'Do you happen to know who they were?'

'There were two gentlemen called Clériot who supply wine to my brother-in-law. We dined with them the other evening.'

The innocent couple, from what Hannah had said. 'And the others?'

'A Monsieur and Madame Beynaud, neighbours of the Clériots.'

'From where?'

'Saumur.'

'Did you speak to them last evening?'

'No.'

No point in mentioning the upper room; Hannah'd reported she was as mystified as they were. He moved on to the next point.

'Do you know anyone by the name of Louise?'

Monica's eyebrows lifted at his change of subject, but she made no comment and considered his latest question. 'Not that I can think of.'

Jackson leant forward, remembering the barman's original wording. 'Or that *sounds* like Louise?' he suggested.

'Well, my sister's name is Eloise.'

The two men exchanged quick glances. 'Was she at the View last night?'

'Yes, of course.'

'So she knows Mr Harry Marlow?'

Monica looked at him for a long minute. 'Of course,' she said again.

'Forgive me, but—how well does she know him?'

'Is this pertinent to your inquiries, Chief Inspector?'

'It is.' Or could be.

'Then I must tell you that they were once engaged.'

Wow! Jackson thought jubilantly. Bullseye!

'And they've remained friends?'

'Yes, and their families. Close friends.'

'Your sister is Mrs Teal?' Whose husband took you out to dinner on Monday. Wheels within wheels!

'That's correct.'

'Has she any special interest in the Gallery?'

'Not really, though she's interested in art. She and the Marlows belong to the Arts Appreciation Society.' She paused. 'Why do you ask?'

'I understand she sometimes lunches with Mr Marlow at the wine bar opposite.' Perhaps that would elicit something, he thought, but he was disappointed.

Her hands tightened in her lap but she made no comment.

Webb looked at her averted face, weighing possibilities. The twins had almost certainly seen the plane land. It was also almost certain they were blackmailing someone as a result of that, and that the driver of the hatchback under the trees was that someone. He had asked for the names of all hatchback owners, but a more specialized list would be helpful.

'Do you know of anyone who drives a hatchback, Miss Tovey?'

She didn't disguise her surprise. 'Certainly. More and more people have them nowadays.'

Unfortunately, that was true.

'Could you give me some names?'

'Well, there's my—' she had been about to say fiancé but made a quick substitution—'bank manager, for a start. And my brother-in-law, and one of my nephews, Jeremy Teal, and I think Mr Marlow has one.'

Webb hadn't missed her hesitation. What had she been going to say?

Fishing, he inquired, 'Who is your bank manager, Miss Tovey?' He knew, of course, from the list of contacts they'd had made.

'Mr Latimer at the National in King Street.' She glanced at Jackson, who was writing down the names. 'I'd be grateful, though, if you didn't bother him unless it's really necessary. His mother died last night.'

'I'm sorry.' Now how did she know that? Not common knowledge, surely, among the bank's clients?

'He's a personal friend?' he hazarded, and she held his gaze.

'Yes,' she said baldly.

Fair enough; she'd been very helpful. A discreet withdrawal was indicated.

'Well, we won't take up any more of your time, Miss Tovey. Many thanks for your help.'

'And you will put in a word for Miss Tulip?'

'We'll do our best,' Webb said.

The Maypole restaurant was an inexpensive establishment in the High Street, where the chairs and tables were wicker and the waitresses masqueraded as milkmaids. Theo had chosen it advisedly, knowing none of his friends was likely to be there and that despite its touches of whimsy it provided a decent menu.

Although he was early, Abbie was there before him. She raised a hand to attract his attention, and he strolled over to her and kissed her cheek.

'Been waiting long?'

'I was early.' In fact, she'd skipped the last lesson.

'Have you looked at the menu?'

'Not yet.'

Theo summoned one with a lordly gesture and they chose what they would eat. He also ordered a bottle of vin rosé, hoping he wasn't corrupting a minor or whatever. But she'd been drinking wine last night.

As the waitress moved away, he smiled at Abbie. He'd had plenty of time now to work out his story and he saw no reason why she should not accept it. Before he launched into it, though, he wanted to be sure exactly what she had seen. The less embroidery he had to do, the better.

'Now to the object of this exercise,' he began, and she smiled back, though guardedly. 'Exactly what was it you saw when you were playing detective?'

'I saw you meet this Christine girl and kiss her, and then she gave you something.'

Damn! 'And what were you doing in the park?'

'Taking a break from revision.'

'Which you seem to do with alarming frequency. I hope your grades won't suffer.'

'Don't change the subject, Theo. Why did you pretend not to know each other?'

Theo launched into his spiel. 'It's all rather embarrassing, actually. I met Christine at a party, and we flirted a little, as one does. But unfortunately she took rather a shine to me, and her boyfriend wasn't pleased. It was all rather a drag.'

He flashed her his most disarming smile, confident she'd sympathize with Christine's weakness.

'That's all?'

'Dearest Abbie, what more do you want? Her boyfriend

was there last night, hence our discretion.' It had sounded convincing enough in the shower.

'But if he wasn't pleased at your flirting, he must have known you'd met.'

A bit too sharp, this one. 'It was some time ago. We hoped he'd forgotten and didn't want to risk reminding him.'

'Then what was it she gave you in the park?'

'Some letters I'd been silly enough to write her. We thought it better not to leave them lying around.'

'Couldn't she just have burned them?'

'Who has a fire in this weather?' He shook his head sadly. 'You know, you're making me feel as if I'm in the dock.'

The waitress returned with their order, and he was glad of the interruption. It had been trickier than he'd bargained for. However, it seemed that Abbie'd accepted the story, because after a moment she nodded and said, 'OK.'

'Satisfied?'

'Yes. She's not really your girlfriend, then?'

In that at least he could be truthful. 'No, of course not. You know me, foot-loose and fancy-free.'

'Um,' she said, and, abandoning her inquisition, turned her attention to the meal.

An hour later, back in the office, Theo knocked on one of the partner's doors.

'Complications, I'm afraid, sir.'

The man behind the desk looked up. 'Come in, Theo. What is it?'

'You know I've been playing along the girl at Darley Smythe?'

'Of course. That was very interesting information you obtained last week.'

'Unfortunately, sir, we were spotted.'

'What?'

Theo said hastily, 'No, no, it's nothing to worry about. Just that a young girl I know happened to be in the park and saw our meeting. I think I've managed to fob her off, but it would be as well to back off for a bit. Especially since Christine was getting a bit too keen anyway, if you see what I mean.'

The disingenuous comment didn't fool the man behind the desk. Thought a lot of himself, did young Teal. Well, he was a personable young man, and if his looks opened doors that were usually closed to them, fair enough. In industrial espionage, he thought wryly, you played the cards you were dealt.

'Very well, Theo, I leave it to your discretion. Keep me posted.'

'Yes, sir, I will.' And Theo left his office, closing the door on a sigh of relief.

CHAPTER 13

By lunch-tine Claudia could stand it no longer, and, leaving a note for Abbie on the hall table, she drove round to the Teals' house. Eloise's car was in the drive, and it was she who opened the door.

'Claudia, hello! Come in; I've just got back myself.'

Claudia silently followed her into the house, rehearsing in her mind what she wanted to say.

'Have you eaten?' Eloise was asking, leading the way into the sitting-room.

'No, I'm—not hungry.'

'Nor am I; it's this infernal heat. Let's have a nice long G & T on the terrace. It's shaded there at this time of day.' With practised speed she mixed the drinks and carried them outside, setting them down on a table close to a hammock and a group of garden chairs. Claudia chose the hammock, subconsciously seeking the comforting rhythms of childhood at this moment of crisis.

'Have you been back to the Gallery this morning?' Eloise asked, sipping her drink. 'I meant to pop in, but didn't get round to it. I should think Harry's delighted with all those sales last night.'

'Yes.' Claudia laid her glass carefully on the table. 'Eloise, I think I should tell you that I know you and Harry have been lovers ever since we were married.'

'Oh, my dear,' Eloise said, 'I'm so sorry.' It was as though she'd suffered a bereavement, Claudia thought. And perhaps she had.

'But we're not really lovers, you know,' Eloise went on gently. 'Just old and close friends who very occasionally go to bed together.'

She made it sound so reasonable, as though Claudia were making a fuss.

'Does Justin know?'

'I shouldn't think so; he's never mentioned it.' She paused. 'Are you proposing to tell him?'

'I imagine he'll find out, when I file for divorce.'

Eloise was very still. Her spectacle lenses had darkened in the sunshine, hiding the expression in her eyes. Perhaps it was as well.

'You intend to?'

'Are you surprised? Have you no conception of how I feel? My husband and my best friend—it's one of the oldest clichés. I knew you'd loved each other once, but that was years ago. I *trusted* you!' She heard the self-pity in her voice, but was powerless to suppress it.

'I'm really very sorry, Claudia. We didn't intend you to find out.'

'That I can believe.'

The telephone shrilled in the room behind them and Eloise went to answer it. Claudia heard her say, 'Oh, it's you. Claudia's here.' And then, 'Yes, I was out all morning.'

Harry must have tried to phone earlier to warn her. Whatever they now said to each other, she didn't want to hear it. She stood up quickly and walked down to the lawn. An automatic sprinkler was sweeping the garden in slow, mesmerizing arcs, its fine spray glinting in the sunshine. She seemed to be watching it for a long time before Eloise returned to the terrace. She supposed they'd been planning their course of action.

Since Eloise made no move to come down and join her, Claudia went back up the steps.

'Harry, I presume.'

'Yes.' Eloise sat down and reached for her glass. After a moment she said, 'We've decided to end it.'

'Why?'

'We couldn't go on hurting you.'

'Very noble, but the gesture comes too late.'

'Claudia, please don't do anything rash. At the moment you're hurt and angry—rightly so, but do think things out carefully before making a decision.' She added quietly, 'Harry's distraught—he doesn't know what to do.'

Claudia leant back under the canopy, closing her eyes against the brightness. The decision to come here had taken more out of her than she'd realized, and she felt drained. If only she could sleep, and wake to find it was all a nightmare. But almost immediately the sound of the doorbell jerked her eyes open again.

'For heaven's sake!' Eloise exclaimed irritably. 'What now?'

A ring round the Shillingham hotels revealed where the Beynauds had spent the night, but unfortunately the birds had flown: quite literally flown, having left for Paris on the early morning flight. It had therefore been too late to alert either British or French Customs, a fact which caused Webb considerable frustration. All he could do was pass their names to Interpol and hope that anything they might have purchased at the Gallery would still be in their possession by the time the necessary warrants came through.

If, of course, they had purchased anything. There was no proof, and Marlow had been quite plausible. Yet surely the abortive approach to the Frenchmen—not to mention Dilys Hayward's unceremonious removal from the passage— must have some significance.

'We'll go and see that manager this evening,' he told

Jackson as they finished their lunch. 'At home this time, without Marlow to back him up. If anything shady's going on, he'll be the weak link in the chain.' He pushed back his chair. 'In the meantime, lad, we're off to Hatherley. It's time we met Mrs Eloise Teal and found out what she can tell us about the Gallery.'

He was surprised, when she opened the door to them, at the contrast between her and her sister. Though both were good-looking women, there was little family resemblance between them, Mrs Teal being considerably taller and more striking, despite—or even because of—the enormous spectacles through which she was now regarding them. He had a feeling—no more than a nebulous stirring of the atmosphere—that for some reason she was on edge. In which case, he thought with satisfaction, their visit was well timed.

'Come through,' she said resignedly, when he identified himself. They followed her into the hall with its Chinese rugs and porcelain vases and through a luxuriously appointed sitting-room to the terrace outside, where another woman was sitting rocking gently in a hammock.

'This is Mrs Marlow,' Eloise said. 'The police, Claudia.'

Webb registered Ken's quick glance. Were they about to put the cat among the pigeons? He hoped not, but the stakes were too high not to play such cards as he held. He nodded to Mrs Marlow and something in her manner resurrected his *frisson* of awareness. She, too, was tense. What had they interrupted here?

'Sit down, Chief Inspector,' Eloise said tersely. 'Can I get you a cold drink?'

'Thank you, no, we've just finished lunch.' He seated himself on one of the comfortable padded chairs and Jackson did the same. 'I understand you're something of an art buff, Mrs Teal? We were at the Gallery this morning.'

'Oh yes?'

Claudia looked at her quickly. Had Harry mentioned that on the phone?

'You belong to an art society, don't you?'

'That's right; so does my friend here.'

'And her husband,' Webb said.

A pause, then: 'Yes,' Eloise acknowledged.

'I'm interested in art myself; perhaps I should think of joining. What does it involve?'

'Lectures, visits to cathedrals, that kind of thing.'

'Do your visits ever take you abroad?'

'Sometimes, on special tours.'

'When was your last trip, Mrs Teal?'

She said impatiently, 'I really don't see why this should concern you, but we went to Portugal at the beginning of April.'

Claudia spoke for the first time. 'Why did you go to my husband's Gallery, Chief Inspector?'

'We've been checking up on some French tourists,' he improvised, watching her closely. 'We suspected they were at the Private View last night, but their names weren't on the guest list.'

'We often have gate-crashers. Short of posting someone on the door, it's unavoidable.'

He tried the same ploy he'd used with her husband. 'What was on display upstairs?'

She looked surprised. 'Nothing; that room's not open to the public.'

'But I understood several people went up there?'

She shook her head. 'It could only have been to the cloakroom.'

There were three possibilities: first, she knew nothing. Second, there was nothing to know and they were barking up the wrong tree. Third, something was going on, but Marlow had tipped her off.

'You didn't go up there yourself last evening, either of you?'

Eloise Teal shook her head and Mrs Marlow said, 'Of course not.'

'I also asked your husband about his window-cleaners,' Webb added with apparent inconsequence. Claudia gazed at him blankly, and he went on, 'He didn't seem to know he'd been employing the two young men who were murdered last week.'

'Really? How awful.'

'Were you aware of that, Mrs Teal?' Webb asked casually.

'I? How should I know who cleans the Gallery windows?'

'I thought they might have called during one of your visits.' He held her eyes for a long moment, and it was hers which fell first. In his heart he apologized to the woman on the hammock, who had now ceased her rocking.

'In fact both of you have a tenuous link with the murders. The victims also cleaned your husband's premises, Mrs Teal, and of course their bodies were found by your mother's house.'

Eloise said jerkily, 'That was coincidence, thank God. My sister had a very worrying few days, after seeing that man.'

'I realize that. I called on her this morning, too.'

'You're having a busy day, Chief Inspector.'

'Indeed, and it's not over yet.' He stood up and moved to the open patio door, surveying the room within. 'What a beautiful home you have. May I have a quick look at your pictures on my way out?'

She did not reply and he stepped inside. While the Badderleys' house also had its share of treasures, they had been displayed indiscriminately, piled on every available surface. Here, due care had been taken to give each superb piece sufficient space. Webb moved slowly round the room, studying the exquisite watercolours which lined it and pausing to admire in turn early Broadshire porcelain, crystal, a collection of ivory. He came to a final halt in front of a piece of mosaic mounted on the wall, a two-foot-square representation of Virgin and Child, and felt the hairs in the nape of his neck rise. If this was what he thought it was—

As he bent forward to examine it more closely, he was aware that Mrs Teal and Jackson had followed him into the room.

'This is magnificent,' he said without turning. 'Where did you come across it?'

'Oh, I keep my eyes open wherever I go.'

'Any more like this?'

'No, unfortunately it's the only one.'

Jackson was standing beside her, alert but uncomprehending. Search warrants, Webb was thinking; they'd need to go over this house and the Marlows', plus the Gallery and the manager's home. He could only hope neither Teal nor Miss Tovey was on the Bench this afternoon.

Though he gave no sign of it, a feeling of excitement, of a solution almost in sight, was building up in him. A session with his sketchpad might well clinch it; frequently, unseen links materialized when he was able to commit to paper the people and places that figured in a case.

Meanwhile, his unwilling hostess was waiting to show him to the door, and reluctantly he allowed her to do so.

Jackson could hardly contain his curiosity until they were in the car. 'What on earth was all that about, Guv? I know you like painting, but going on about societies and visits abroad and all. What were you getting at?'

'Just a moment, Ken.' Webb reached for the car phone and dialled Carrington Street, detailing his requirements while Jackson listened in growing bewilderment.

'We're going to search that house? The home of a magistrate?' he asked in awe as Webb rang off. 'But—why? Did I miss something? Was there evidence of drugs?'

'No, I reckon we've been on the wrong track there. But what's the *second* biggest smuggling racket these days, Ken?'

'Stolen artefacts,' Jackson said slowly.

'Right. And worth over a billion dollars at the last count.'

'You really think that's what they're up to?'

'I think it's what *someone*'s up to, but I'm not sure who. That mosaic on the wall, for instance; I'm willing to bet it was smuggled out of Cyprus, and if I'm right it's virtually priceless. Which is why we're going to sit here until the support group arrives to cordon off the house. Can't have our prime exhibit walking, now can we?'

He pushed back the car seat and stretched out his legs. 'I was reading about the trade in mosaics the other day;

they're ripped out of churches in northern Cyprus virtually to order. Since they're both Greek and Christian, the Turks make no attempt to protect them.'

Jackson whistled. 'And this was what the White twins stumbled on? No wonder they bit the dust.'

'Yes, but who despatched them, Ken? And have those two women back there any idea of what's involved? I very much doubt it.'

Jackson sat in silence for some minutes. Then he said, 'So that's why you were asking about foreign trips.'

'Contacts and so on. It'd fit, wouldn't it?'

'Then the goods are flown over secretly and offered for sale in that room at the Gallery?'

'If we're on the right track. But it seems incredibly dicey to conduct business of that kind while two hundred people are milling about downstairs.'

Monica called round to see George on the way home from work, as arranged. He'd not been into the bank that day, and greeted her looking less formal than usual in an open-neck shirt.

In view of Mrs Latimer's hostility she had been to the house only a couple of times, but it seemed still to have the aura of the dead woman. The chair in which Monica had last seen her still bore the indentations of her body, and a silk shawl was draped over the arm as though temporarily laid aside. Monica wondered if the house was to become a shrine with everything remaining as the owner had left it— her book on the table, her clothes in the drawer. But surely not; George had been fond of his mother, but he was essentially a realist.

As though reading her thoughts, he said, 'I haven't acclimatized myself yet. This is still very much Mother's house.'

'Will you stay on here?' Monica tried to keep her voice neutral.

'Good lord no, I'll sell it. It doesn't hold particularly happy memories.'

So much for the mausoleum.

'Don't think too harshly of her,' he added. 'Things would have been very different if my father had lived.'

'I know; I wish I'd known her better.' It was true; she felt he needed to speak of his mother with someone who'd known and understood her.

For some minutes they discussed the funeral arrangements and other depressing trappings of death. Then, refilling their glasses, George said firmly, 'Now, enough of all that. Tell me about the Private View. Was Jeremy there?'

'Yes, why?'

'I saw him at Gianino's the other evening, with a couple of rather strange characters he carefully didn't introduce.'

'How mysterious.' She went on to tell him about the pictures she was interested in buying and the mutual friends who'd been at the View.

'And we finished up at the wine bar over the road,' she ended, 'which was very pleasant.'

'We?'

'Hannah, Gwen, Dilys and I. I phoned you from there, but you were still at the hospital.'

He nodded. 'By the way, an odd thing happened this afternoon; a couple of Bobbies came round and asked what I'd been doing on the evening of the twenty-first.'

The significance of the date was not lost on Monica. 'Why you, for goodness sake?'

'They assured me it was a routine inquiry, but they were uncommonly interested in the car and examined it very carefully. Lord knows what they were looking for.'

'Oh, George, I'm sorry—I'm afraid that was my fault. Mr Webb asked me this morning who I knew with hatchbacks and I mentioned you among others. But I did ask him not to bother you unless it was necessary.'

'He must have thought it was. Anyway, since my social life runs on very circumscribed lines, I was able to satisfy them I'd spent the evening here with Mother. Betsy confirmed it.'

'That's something, I suppose.' She added with a smile, 'Still, you'll be considerably less circumscribed in future.'

He looked across at her. 'Yes; Monica, there's something I have to say, and this seems as good a time as any.'

'My goodness, that sounds solemn. What is it?'

'I don't want you to think that now Mother's died, you're going to be rushed straight into marriage.'

She said only half-humorously, 'You've changed your mind?' and surprised in herself an acute anxiety. It would be rich indeed if after all her private reservations, George now turned the tables and released her from her promise. Especially when she was coming round to realizing it was what she wanted after all.

'I think you may have changed yours,' he answered her. 'You've been wonderfully patient over the last four years— perhaps a little too patient.' He gave a difficult smile. 'What I'm trying to say is, I don't want you to feel tied down. If you'd rather continue on a more casual basis, I can accept that.'

Perhaps, Monica thought, his mother's disapproval had been a safety-net for him too. Now it had been removed, he might have taken fright.

'Is that what you want?' she asked, and was humbled to find how much hung on his reply.

'No; I want you for my wife, but I've always known your feelings weren't as strong. And why,' he added very quietly.

Monica felt a sense of shock. 'What do you mean?'

'Don't worry, your secret's safe with me.'

She sat very still, not looking at him. He could only be referring to Justin. How long had he known of her feelings in that direction? How long had she? Certainly she'd believed them to be private to herself.

At last she said softly, 'I've been very stupid.'

'No, darling. Eloise took him from you as surely as he took her from Harry.'

'But there was nothing between us.'

'There might have been, in time.'

She looked up, meeting his troubled eyes. 'I'm not in love with Justin, George. There was a time when I might have been, a little, but it was probably only a case of sour grapes.

I can honestly say I have no regrets. I enjoy my life; I didn't realize quite how much till it seemed under threat.'

'And you don't want it to change?'

'Only in one respect; I'd like you to share it with me.'

He released his breath in a long sigh, and a smile spread over his face. 'Nothing would give me more pleasure,' he said.

It was after 7.0 when Webb arrived home. The outcome of the searches had been a great deal of indignation and not much else. Apart from the Cypriot mosaic there had been only a few pieces of doubtful provenance in the Teal household, and even these were debatable since it was possible they'd been purchased legally. The other three premises, despite several hours' diligent searching, had revealed precisely nothing. Webb was not popular. HQ had already received a strongly worded complaint from Mr Justin Teal, JP.

But damn it, he was sure he was on the right track, though he'd realized they were shutting the stable door after the horse had gone. If their search of the Gallery had been twenty-four hours earlier, the result might have been very different.

He let himself into his flat and began to prepare his meal. When his marriage broke up eight years ago he had determined never to live out of tins, and in fact did not possess a tin-opener. Normally he enjoyed cooking, and Hannah maintained that the more involved he was with a case, the more elaborate his cuisine. However, there were rare occasions when he was in a hurry to get the meal over, and this was one of them. As he peeled some potatoes, he acknowledged that baked beans would have been a useful stand-by.

Throughout the preparation and eating of his meal, his thoughts continued to circle round the people he'd been speaking to that day, their hesitations, their evasions, their unease. Something was stirring at the back of his mind, and he was impatient to get it down on paper.

As soon as he'd finished, he went to the living-room and set up his easel. Then he paused. It was stuffy in there, despite the open window, but though he preferred to work outdoors, it was too much effort, after all the comings and goings of the day, to set out again now.

Then a compromise presented itself; he'd work in the garden. It was communal to all twelve flats in the building, and he seldom made use of it. Abandoning easel and paints, he collected instead sketchpad, crayons and canvas chair and went down the two flights of stairs and round the side of the house.

The garden was deserted, which suited him very well. The grass was crisp under his feet and as he crossed it, he wondered when they'd have rain. It was only the end of May; early in the summer to face a drought.

Beyond the lawn lay the wild area, a wilderness of shrubs and bushes which had been left untended to encourage wildlife. Webb set his chair up in front of it, alongside the small pond. To his right the sun hung low in the sky. He'd an hour or more of daylight still, which should be enough for his purpose.

Quickly, with light, sure strokes, he began to sketch in the background to the crime; first, the deserted stretch of the Chipping Claydon road with, marked along its length, the house Frank Andrews had visited and the Mulberry Bush pub. To the right of the sheet he drew a broken line representing the cross-country road to Chedbury and that other pub, the Magpie, where the twins were last seen alive. On the far left, a square denoted the Badderleys' house and, down the road from it, a wood behind which he drew in a small aircraft. Then he sat back, staring at the layout. After a minute or two he inserted the van in the lay-by, and, under trees, the hatchback car.

Justin Teal had a hatchback, so did one of his sons, George Latimer the bank manager, and Harry Marlow. All of them had been asked to account for their movements and at first glance all appeared to have alibis. Those alibis were now being rechecked.

Tearing off the top sheet, he started to people the next one with the actors in the drama: the identical twins in their green tracksuits, the members of their gang, Mr and Mrs Trubshaw, the Hargreaves. Had any of them said anything which could be regarded in a different light? Had there been any discrepancies? The little figures were surprisingly lifelike and he studied each in turn, assessing what he knew or guessed of their characters.

Monica Tovey was there because the bodies had been found near her house. Then there was her sister, who owned the mosaic; the Marlows, and the softly spoken Tony Reid. Webb had not after all been able to interview him this evening; immediately after the search he had left the house and no one knew where he had gone. They'd catch up with him at the Gallery tomorrow.

Finally, little stick figures, each in its own identifying colour, were inserted into the position where, according to their statements, they'd been between 9.0 p.m. and midnight on 21st May. Could this one—or that—have got from A to B and back again in time to commit murder?

The sun disappeared behind the houses and a small breeze ruffled the papers on the grass beside him. Looking up, he saw that a light had gone on in Hannah's window. He wondered whether she had looked out and seen him. Realizing he was working, she would not have disturbed him.

He straightened, easing his back. Well, there they were, the basic ingredients of a crime. One of these pleasant, civilized people must have perpetrated it, must in fact be not only a murderer but the mastermind behind the extremely daring and brazen organization which was robbing countries of their antiquities and selling them at vast profit. If the Gallery was implicated Harry Marlow seemed the best bet, but they had no proof that it was. And Justin Teal, in whose house the mosaic rested, was as yet an unknown quantity. He would certainly merit investigation.

CHAPTER 14

As Monica drove past the house on her way to the garage she saw Justin's car parked outside, and he was in the hall to meet her as she came in from the garden.

'Hello, there; are you waiting for me?'

'I am, yes. Your mother's out.'

'I know, they're having a social at the bridge club. Come through.'

'You're late yourself; have you been preparing for the sales?'

'No, I went to see George.'

'Ah. I must drop him a line. How is he?'

'Fine. Are you on your way home?'

'No,' he said, his voice tightening, 'I've been home most of the afternoon. Eloise sent for me.'

'She's not ill?' For a panic-stricken moment Monica wondered if she'd misjudged her sister's state of health, as she had Mrs Latimer's.

'She's well enough, but considerably upset. The police have been turning the house over.'

'*What?*'

'Exactly. Imagine the Bench's reaction to a search-warrant for my house. The police are going to hear more about this, I can tell you.'

'Was it to do with the car? They called to ask George about his.'

'They looked at it, certainly, along with everything else. My God, what the hell did they imagine—'

'Justin, wait a minute. Have you met the Chief Inspector?'

'Only in Court.'

'He's a man who knows what he's doing. There must be some reason—'

He interrupted her. 'Oh, there was a reason, so-called— that knick-knack on the sitting-room wall. Religious artefacts aren't my scene, but it's inoffensive enough and if Eloise wants to hang it there, I'm not having the police trying to stop her.'

'The mosaic, you mean? What's the matter with it?'

'I've no idea. They were asking all sorts of questions and they've taken it away with them, together with a few other trinkets. If they so much as *hint* they're stolen property, I swear I'll take the lot of them to Court.'

'What other things did they take?'

He shrugged. 'A few pieces of jewellery, that carved statue from the landing and a couple of the stone vases from the hall alcove.'

'Did they say why they wanted them?'

'To check their provenance, if you please. Bloody nerve!'

She had never seen him so rattled. 'Where *did* they come from?'

'Oh, Eloise picked them up on her travels. Webb saw the mosaic when he called round earlier—that's what started it all.'

'Well, I shouldn't let it bother you. No doubt they'll meekly return everything tomorrow and you won't hear any more about it.'

'*We* might not, but I assure you the police will. The Marlows had their place searched, too.'

Monica frowned, liking the affair less and less. 'Perhaps it's to do with the Arts Society.'

'Quite possibly; when Webb was round earlier he was asking about it, making out he was thinking of joining, and so on.'

'But that wasn't the reason for his visit, surely?'

'No, he was interested in last night's do. According to Claudia, he seemed to think something was going on upstairs.'

Monica had a sudden picture of Tony Reid taking the Clériots on one side, and Dilys saying she'd been hurried back into the Gallery. All at once the whole business had assumed sinister proportions. She glanced at her brother-in-law, who was staring at the carpet and chewing on his lip. No point, though, in adding to his worries with what were, after all, mere suspicions. If something was seriously wrong, he'd know soon enough.

He sighed and rose to his feet. 'Well, I'd better be getting back. I just wanted to talk it over with you and see what you thought.

'By the way,' he added, as she showed him to the door, 'a spot of good news for a change: Jeremy's landed quite a coup; his agency was anxious to get that new Italian tenor on to their books, and he's managed to pull it off. Vittorio Vinetti, his name is.'

'I don't think I've heard of him.'

'Hardly anyone has in this country but it seems he's destined for the top. All the big agencies were after him, so negotiations were very hush-hush. Apparently Jeremy took him and his agent out to dinner to finalize it, and things were just at a delicate stage when old George wandered across. It was all a little embarrassing.'

'I can imagine,' Monica said drily.

He started down the steps, then stopped and turned. 'Talking of George, will you two be getting married now?'

'Yes,' she said.

For a moment longer he looked at her. Then he nodded and went on his way and Monica closed the door.

Tony Reid was alone in the Gallery when Webb and Jackson arrived the next morning. No longer the smooth, self-assured young man of the previous day, he regarded them with unease.

'Mr Marlow's not here,' he said sullenly. The search of his home obviously still rankled.

'It's you we'd like to see,' Webb said pleasantly. 'I think it's time we got things sorted, don't you? Tell me, Mr Reid, why did you kill the White twins?'

The man stared at him wildly. 'Me? I never killed anyone in my life! I didn't even know them!'

'Come now, two nice-looking young men like that? You must have noticed them when they cleaned the windows.'

Reid moistened his lips. 'I might have taken them a mug of tea once or twice.'

'There you are, then. And they recognized you, didn't they?'

His eyes were darting about nervously. 'I don't know what you mean.'

'Saw you by the plane, and recognized you.'

It was a shot in the dark, but it struck deep and true. Reid gasped and his face turned a sickly yellow. 'What—what plane?'

'The one you met on the Steeple Bayliss road on the twelfth of May.'

Reid swallowed convulsively and glanced desperately at the door. 'Please—someone will come in any minute, I really can't—'

Webb nodded to Jackson, who stepped to the door and turned the notice on it from Open to Closed. 'Now we needn't bother about interruptions,' Webb said comfortably. He pulled the chair out from behind the counter. 'Sit down, Mr Reid, and take your time. We're in no hurry.'

The man had begun to whimper. 'It was nothing to do with me; I was only doing my job.'

'Mr Marlow gave the orders?'

A nod.

'And he was with you, was he?'

Another nod.

'When did you realize you'd been spotted?'

'I *didn't*—I mean, we weren't! Everything went off just as usual.'

'It was a regular practice, then?'

Reid muttered something and Webb leant forward. 'Come again?'

'Three or four times a year.'

'And you used the hatchback to load the goods into?'

Another guess.

'Yes.' He was slumped in the chair, his whole attitude one of dejection.

'Your car, or Mr Marlow's?'

'His.'

'Got a hatchback of your own?'

'No, a small saloon.'

'Now for the sixty-four-thousand-dollar question, and that's probably a low estimate. What were you unloading?'

Before he could answer, the door was pushed open and Marlow's voice said angrily, 'Tony, it's nine-fifteen! Why haven't you opened?'

He was into the room before he saw them, since the counter was along the same wall as the door. He stopped short, and the woman behind him bumped into him. It was Eloise Teal.

'Come in, both of you,' Webb said genially, 'we're having a very interesting chat here.'

Tony Reid started out of his chair. 'I didn't tell them anything, Mr Marlow! They—they seemed to know!'

'Shut up!' Marlow turned to Webb. 'For your information, Chief Inspector, I'm filing a complaint of police harassment. Not content with turning over my house and business premises on a whim, you come back here and start badgering my assistant. I was very patient with you yesterday and let you snoop round to your heart's content. And what did you find? Nothing! And that, my friend, is because there's nothing to find. Can you get that into your suspicious mind? Because I've had just about enough of this, and I know Mr Teal feels the same. In fact, he told me he'd already been in touch—'

'Perhaps you'll be good enough to fill in a few gaps for us,' Webb interrupted smoothly. 'We've got as far as your meeting the plane with the hatchback and unloading the goods. I gather they're stolen artefacts, but I'd be grateful for a few more details.'

Eloise gasped. Marlow stared at him, and Jackson, struck by how dark his eyes were, realized it was in contrast to the sudden pallor of his face. After a moment, Marlow rallied.

'What a fertile imagination you have, Chief Inspector. You can't have any evidence for these wild accusations.'

'We also believe,' Webb continued, 'that contacts are

made during your trips abroad with the Arts Society, who, I'm pretty sure, have absolutely no knowledge of what you're up to. And since you fly in planeloads three or four times a year, you must be on to a nice little earner.'

'What's all this nonsense about a plane?' It was a brave try, but his voice had lost its arrogant confidence.

'We've had reports of low-flying aircraft on numerous occasions. On the twelfth of May there were several, plus a complaint from a farmer whose field had been churned up. All in all, you've led us quite a dance.'

Eloise Teal stepped suddenly forward. 'Congratulations, Mr Webb. I never thought you'd crack it.'

Marlow turned sharply, gripping her arm. 'Eloise, don't be a fool! They can't prove a thing!'

'Nonsense, Harry. Apart from dotting the i's and crossing the t's, they're home and dry. We can't complain, you know: we've had six good years, and quite honestly the excitement has worn off anyway.'

'For God's sake listen to me! Don't say anything! You don't know what's involved!'

Tony Reid had been staring at her in amazement. 'You?' he demanded. '*You're* the one he spoke of as The Boss?'

She gave a little laugh. 'Guilty. It was my idea and I masterminded the whole operation.'

She's actually enjoying this, Webb thought in wonder. It was as though, now the game was up, she was trading its stimulation for the notoriety that would follow, eager for the admiration, albeit grudging, which she expected her ingenuity to arouse.

Marlow tried once more. 'Eloise, just let me—' but she shook him off. Behind those large spectacles her eyes were glistening. She leant against the corner of the counter, her arms lightly folded.

'You see, Chief Inspector, I was tired of being written off as a dimwit. Everyone thought Monica had the brains, but she's always had to work harder than I have for what she's wanted. At school she spent all her time studying. I hardly did any work, but I got the same exam results. In fact, I used to sell answers to the other girls—it was quite lucrative.

'Then Monica went into the business but because I was lazy, Father thought I hadn't a brain in my head. I didn't bother to correct him—in any case, I married straight from school. But gradually I felt the need of mental stimulation. That's why I joined the Arts Appreciation Society, and persuaded Harry and Claudia to do the same. As time went on I became very involved with it, chairing committees and helping to arrange trips and outings. And that, as you guessed, was how this business started. I used to go over before every tour to check arrangements, and one night in a restaurant I started chatting to a German couple at the next table. After the meal they invited me back to their home for coffee. And that,' she ended softly, 'was where I saw my first mosaic.'

Marlow, having given up the attempt to stop her, was now leaning against the wall staring down at the floor.

Webb said, 'They were dealers?'

'Yes, Munich's an important centre for that kind of thing. Seeing how interested I was, they told me how to set the whole thing up; you need only a small organization—three or four to obtain the goods, a couple of middle men, and the buyer, which would be me. But I needed someone by me I could trust implicitly, someone I knew I could depend on. And I chose Mr Marlow.'

She glanced at him, but he gave no sign of having heard her.

'It's a fascinating business, Mr Webb. Any place where there's been social upheaval or war is a rich picking-ground —the Lebanon, Greece, Cyprus.' She smiled slightly. 'As you discovered, we didn't confine ourselves to mosaics. We've handled icons, vases, frescoes, coins. Sometimes we sold through auction houses, but mostly to private customers.'

'Who came and viewed them upstairs here?'

'Yes; it's always worked perfectly, but this time we had to change the date at the last minute. An important customer could only come on the evening of the twenty-ninth, and asked us to bring the date forward. Since there was an item he was particularly interested in, we'd little choice. By that time the Private View had been arranged and all the invitations were out. We knew it was risky to combine the two, but it was a challenge and as long as we were careful it should have been all right.' She looked at Reid, who flushed and turned away.

'So what went wrong, Mr Reid?' Webb prompted.

He glanced for guidance at Harry Marlow, who continued to stare at the floor. But after Mrs Teal's speech, he must have felt the time for caution was past. 'My job was to show up the customers—separately, to preserve confidentiality.' His voice took on a defensive tone. 'But Mr Marlow just said "The French couple", and when I heard Miss Tovey talking French to those men, I thought it was them. They shouldn't have been there, anyway. I found out later Mr Teal invited them.' And he looked accusingly at Eloise.

She shrugged. 'Anyway, there you have it, Mr Webb. I don't regret a thing; I've proved what I set out to, that I'm as astute as the rest of the family, and able to play for much higher stakes.'

'Let's hope it'll sustain you over the next few years,' Webb said drily. 'One more point, though; we were closing in, but the thing that clinched it was seeing that mosaic on your wall. Why in the name of goodness did you risk that? If you'd hung it in your bedroom, say, I'd never have seen it.'

'But you miss the point; half the fun was displaying it under everyone's eyes. What enjoyment would there have been in hiding it away?'

It seemed she was as much a gambler as Miss Tulip. 'Well, that's cleared up that side of it; now we come to the more serious part. Tell me, did you meet the plane yourself?'

She frowned, glancing back at Marlow, who still hadn't moved. 'No; Harry needed an assistant, which was why he brought in Tony Reid. I always kept in the background. As you saw, Tony'd no idea I was involved.'

'Right, then it's your turn, Mr Marlow. It was you the twins recognized, wasn't it?'

At last Marlow looked up, his face grey, and Eloise drew in her breath sharply.

'Twins?' she repeated urgently. 'The ones who were killed? That's nothing to do with us!'

Marlow said flatly, 'I did tell you to keep quiet.'

'But—' she glanced wildly from him to Webb, the pride she had shown in her enterprise abruptly fading.

'Let me tell you what happened, Mrs Teal, since Mr Marlow seems reluctant to. He can correct me if I'm wrong. The first fact to establish is that the Whites cleaned the Gallery windows, along with many other business premises in town. And not unnaturally they'd seen Mr Marlow here.'

'But I don't—'

He lifted a hand and she fell silent. 'They had two principal interests in life, football and burglary. On Saturday May the twelfth they'd been to Steeple Bayliss for the last match of the season, which I think I'm right in saying Shillingham won. They stayed on to celebrate after the other supporters had left, and when they eventually did set off for home, they happened to see an invitingly empty house, which they naturally stopped to burgle. All in all, they must have thought they'd had a most satisfactory day. But then things went disastrously wrong, though at first it would have seemed the opposite.'

He paused, looking round at the intent faces. 'So far we've been dealing with fact. Now we come to conjecture, but I reckon it's pretty close to the mark. As they were driving along with their loot, they noticed a plane flying very low overhead, and realized it was in fact about to land behind the small wood which lined the road. So they stopped and went to see what was going on. Two men had met the plane and were engaged in unloading its cargo into their hatchback car. Now, this is the bit I'm not sure about. I doubt if the boys broke cover, and the marks of the plane are some fifty yards from the edge of the wood where they were presumably hiding. It was a full moon, but even so it would be relatively difficult to recognize someone they didn't know well from that distance. Therefore—and I'm guessing now—I think one of the men—Mr Marlow—went over to the edge of the wood for some reason?'

He ended interrogatively, and, getting no response from Marlow, raised an eyebrow at Reid, who slowly nodded.

'The moonlight might have been on his face, but anyway the twins saw him and recognized him as one of their customers. And though they didn't know what he was doing, it was plain enough he shouldn't have been doing it. So they decided to try a spot of blackmail.'

Eloise said aridly, 'Harry, is this true?'

He raised his shoulders in a resigned shrug.

'I think, Mr Marlow,' Webb said mildly, 'that it's time you took some part in this discussion. But before you do, I must caution you that—'

'Save your breath,' Marlow said harshly. 'I've already told you I've an alibi for the night of the murder.'

'Yes, we've been checking up on that. You told us, and your wife corroborated, that you'd been to the Grand Theatre together, arrived home soon after ten and settled in for the night.'

'That's plain enough, isn't it?'

'What you didn't tell us, and we didn't realize till we went back to your wife last evening, is that when you reached home she went straight up to bed and you remained downstairs.'

'As I do every night; she always goes up first, and I have a nightcap and read the paper or watch television for another hour or so.'

'Yes, she told us that too. But that particular evening she was tired and fell asleep almost at once. She wouldn't have heard you if you left the house again.'

Eloise said just above a whisper, '*Did* you do it, Harry? Did you murder those boys?'

He raised a haggard face. 'It was as much for your sake as mine, darling. You know what blackmailers are—one payment is never enough. And we'd been so careful, covered our tracks so well. It didn't seem right that two cocky little upstarts should ruin it all.' He paused. 'Not that I realized there were two of them—or even who they were. The note gave nothing away. It simply said if I wanted my connection with the plane and its cargo kept quiet, to leave a suitcase containing two thousand pounds in the Wood Green lay-by at eleven o'clock on Monday the twenty-first.'

He leant back against the wall, his hands in his pockets. 'It arrived on the Saturday morning, and I can tell you I had a pretty lousy weekend. At first I considered paying up and hoping for the best. But George Latimer's my bank manager—he'd have wondered what was going on. And basically I didn't see why the blackmailer should get away with it. So I got out an old suitcase and stuffed it full of newspapers. The theatre visit was already planned, and it helped to fill in the evening as well as providing an alibi. Or it should have done,' he added grimly.

'So at the appropriate time I went to the lay-by, dumped the suitcase and drove off again. But not far. I parked under some overhanging trees and made my way back, not along the road but through the shrubs and trees which brought me out at the back of the lay-by. Then I lay low and waited.'

'You'd taken a weapon with you?' Webb put in.

'Yes, a kitchen knife.'

Eloise Teal gave a choked sob and put her hand to her mouth, her huge eyes staring at him.

'Well, after a couple of minutes the van drove in and doused its lights. A man jumped down and came running towards the case, which was just in front of where I was hidden. My eyes had adjusted to the dark and I could see him quite clearly—young, fair, and wearing a tracksuit. For a moment I was incapable of moving. Then I forced myself to lunge forward and before he could stop himself he ran straight on to the knife.'

He looked at Webb, remembered horror in his eyes. 'That was bad enough, but what happened next was a nightmare. I *knew* I'd killed him—he was lying on the ground at my feet—but suddenly there he was again, still rushing towards me. I honestly thought I'd gone mad. Then this second figure skidded to a halt, flung back his head and screamed "Gary!"'

He shuddered and unconsciously put his hands over his ears as if to blot out the memory.

'And then?' Webb prompted.

Marlow straightened, his arms falling to his sides. 'Then he just—dropped to the ground. I stood staring at him for some time, still thinking I was hallucinating. But when he didn't move I went over to him, the knife at the ready, and as soon as I reached him I could see he was dead, too. It was—eerie. More terrifying than the first death, which I'd steeled myself for.'

He drew a deep breath. 'Well, I couldn't leave them lying there in full view from the road. I was wearing gloves, of course, so I opened the back of the van and dragged them inside. I saw then that they were only boys, and as alike as two peas. No wonder I'd thought I was seeing double.' He shook his head as though to clear it. 'I covered them with a tarpaulin I found in the van and closed the doors again. Then I collected the suitcase and returned by way of the bushes to the car.

'As you can imagine, I spent the next day waiting for the evening paper and listening to the radio, but there was nothing. And that evening—' he turned to Eloise—'we went to your house for dinner. And to my horror Monica started talking about a dirty green van that had arrived outside her house in the middle of the night. I was petrified. How I didn't give myself away, I'll never know. I was convinced she must know what was in the back, and that I was responsible. And I couldn't begin to imagine how the van had got from the lay-by to North Park.' He drew a deep, shuddering breath. 'So there you have it. In a way it's a relief that it's over.'

For several long minutes no one spoke. Then Eloise said shakily, 'It was all supposed to be a game. If I hadn't involved you in my machinations, this would never have happened. Oh God, Harry!'

Stiffly he put an arm round her. Tony Reid had risen to

his feet, and they all stood unmoving while the three different charges were made.

'The car's just outside,' Webb ended, gesturing them towards the door. In silence they moved together out of the Gallery, Marlow automatically pausing to lock both doors behind them. As they turned towards the police car, a woman came hurrying along the pavement and caught at Harry's arm.

'Oh Mr Marlow, I'm not too late to catch you? I wanted to confirm I'll have that painting I was considering.'

'Thank you, Mrs Grant,' he said heavily. 'Someone'll be in touch.'

'I thought the exhibition was open all week?'

'There's been a change of plan,' he said, and climbed into the back of the car. The woman was still staring after him as it drove away.